My Sunday Drives

Drives

The First Glance into Time

DVINE DMENSIONS
Houston, TX

Coming Soon

from Yolanda Dean

My Sunday Drives Vol. 2

&

Clothed in the Word

Just me and "Bubba"...

When he stopped talking, he moved a step closer to me and spit tobacco directly onto my right cheek. Now, spitting is a nasty thing to begin with but you add chewed up tobacco to it and that makes it downright *disgusting*.

I was frozen in stunned amazement and something inside of me clicked. Something inside of me opened up and I knew that I was about to take the path that could lead to a major breakthrough in understanding or to destruction. And, at that moment either one was just fine with me...

My Sunday Drives

The First Glance into Time

Yolanda Dean

Unless noted, all scripture quotations are from taken from the New King James Version. Copyright © 1979, 1980, 1982 by Thomas Nelson, Inc. Used by permission. All rights reserved.

My Sunday Drives: The First Glance into Time
Copyright © 2012 by Yolanda Dean

Published by DVINE DMENSIONS
Houston, Texas
better.me.publishing@gmail.com

ISBN-10: 0983405670
ISBN-13: 978-0983405672

Cover Design: Better-Me Publishing (In House)
Stock Image © *Jason Yoder* – Fotolia.com

DVINE DMENSIONS is an imprint of **Better-Me Publishing**.

Printed in the United States of America.

CONTENTS

CHAPTER
1

CHAPTER
1

NEVER INSULT
A WOMAN OF GOD!

As I One Sunday morning I awoke with a hunger for something new and exciting and what I stumbled upon has forever changed my view of this world. Instead of getting into my car and driving to church as usual, I decided to don a pair of jeans and a tee shirt, load up with juice and goodies and just drive until I came upon whatever it was I was looking for.

Well, I had been driving for about four hours and was getting a little restless and tired when I came upon this gas station that looked so old I couldn't believe it! It still had the red round pumps, and the attendant who came out and took care of putting the gas in your car as well as washing your windows and checking your oil.

When he saw my brand new BMW he was a little set back because he'd never seen one before. He put my gas in but upon lifting the hood of the car, couldn't find the oil dipstick. When I got out showing him he just looked at me in amazement but said nothing. You see, I had on some brand new Lee "Silver Tab" jeans, some Air Jordans and a tee shirt that said, "The Black Woman - Mother of the Earth." He watched as I showed him and then asked where I was headed with a little concern in his voice.

I looked him up and down and then pulled my shades off to look him dead in the eyes. I said I was from Orlando and was just out on a Sunday drive, looking for something new and exciting. He said that I should be careful and that he thought I should drive about four more miles, take a right on the County Road Highway 420. To just keep driving, that I would find what I was looking for. I thanked him, paid for my gas and got back in my car with a smile and a sigh. "Gee,' I said as I pulled onto the road, 'these kinds of gas stations still exist." Then I shrugged and kept driving.

Exactly four miles down the road I saw County Road Highway 420 and took a right. The scenery became dense and very green. The road soon proved to be the beginning of an interesting journey. As I passed a sign that read "Limon County Parish", I couldn't ever remember seeing that on any map and suddenly became excited that I had found just what I was looking for.

The first thing I saw on my right was the County Christian Church. It looked to have been built back in the 20's yet it was as white and clean, as if they had just put it up yesterday. To my great astonishment, church was just letting out and I saw little boys and girls running outside into the sun to play before heading home for dinner. The strange thing to me was they were all white, not a black face in the parking lot.

I pulled off to the side of the road and watched a little while longer. Surely, in this integrated era of the 21st Century, there was going to be a black face coming through those doors any minute now. After about 10 minutes, I gave up and pulled back onto C. R. Highway 420.

As I drove a bit further, I saw a road to my left just beyond the church called Parish Road. I decided to take that left and before I went any further I immediately pulled out my notepad and hand-held recorder so that I wouldn't get lost back in this place that time had surely passed by.

The first place I came upon was a little white house, or what used to be white but now looked yellow in color. There was an old black man sitting on the porch and I waved to him. He looked up at me and my car and just stopped fanning and let his mouth hang open.

I pulled over to talk with him since he was the first black person I'd seen in this place and he looked very polite but stern. As I got out of my car and he got a chance to really look at me, he began to shake his head and wave me away. I walked over anyway.

"Good Morning," I said as cheerfully as possible. "It sure is nice to feel that breeze. I've been driving all morning and you are the first person that I've wanted to introduce myself to."

He just looked at me and said, "Mornin'".

"My name is Yolanda and I just wanted to ask you how long you've been living here and what it's like here. It seems kind of quiet (that was putting it mildly) and I just wanted to talk with someone. I'm from Orlando and I just felt like driving today!"

He looked past me for a moment and then after making an attempt at fanning himself he answered me with a question. "Chile, how ole you?"

My eyebrows raised and I gave him a look that said you never ask a lady her age. "In my thirties. Why?"

He started shaking his head and laughing and said to me, "The best advice I got fo' you is to get back in that fancy car you got over yonda and head home. You way outta place back in de Parish and I don't think you got sense 'nough to know it."

To say that I was insulted and mad would be putting it lightly. "What is your name sir?" I asked in a very offended voice.

"Limon, Pastor Jonah Petersburg Limon. I'm de pastor at de Limon Parish chuch 'bout 3 miles down dis road. I was born April 15, 1820. I done seen more in dis life den I care to remember."

Well, I thought, at least we now had three things in common - we were both black, we were both ministers, and we were still living!

"Well, Pastor Limon, I'm very glad to meet you. I'm a minister of the gospel myself and it is an honor to meet a soldier of the Lord of your stature. So, what is Limon County Parish like? Are the people friendly? Have you had any of those nasty storms we've been having lately?" I was doing my best to be personable and likeable.

Pastor Limon suddenly grunted, sat a little straighter in his seat and was very quiet looking off to his right. I turned my head to see what I was missing and I caught a glimpse of a police car that looked as if it had been borrowed from the Andy Griffith show.

I was shading my eyes because I had taken off my sun glasses but I distinctly saw a middle aged white man in uniform with the top buttons undone, his white cotton tee shirt showing and he was staring at me and my car. I put my sun glasses back on and started to wave but Pastor Limon said, "Stay still, chile. Just stay still." So, I did.

After a few minutes the police car turned the corner and passed the house; with a tilt of his head he acknowledged our existence. "Why must I have stayed still?" I asked. "He's only a deputy looks like and he looked nice enough."

"You rally is young an stupid ain't cha?"

That was enough to make me leave his porch and return to my Sunday ride. I've been called a lot of things throughout my thirty something years but young and stupid were the insults to top it all off. Here I was trying to be friendly, with a man of God no less, and he was calling me stupid! What was this? With a look meant to wither the strongest of men, I stood up and started to leave the porch when an old leathery hand caught me by the arm.

"Sit down a minute chile'. I want to let you know 'bout a few things fo' you git yo'self in some serious trouble."

I looked at him with insulted yet cold eyes and took a seat in the old rusted chair next to him.

"Listen, Limon County Parish been de same since I was born. De people here are still just as backwards as they always been an I do mean it. We still have to get up every mornin' at de crack of dawn an go on down to de fields and plant or harvest. We still got to say "Mornin' Mr. Charlie Sir" just like you probably done read 'bout in some book since you look so young an careless. We don't drive 'roun in hot lil cars like dat. Nope, we either ride a horse, walk, or pray dat someone come along in an ole beat up Ford. An, I don't care what you think; there's nothin' better on de road den a 1920 Ford Roadster Pickup! No, Sir - nothin' better.''

I jumped in, "Wait a minute, Pastor Limon. Don't the children go to school? Don't you all have any type of rights around here? My Lord, Martin Luther King, Jr. must be totally unheard of here or just ignored!"

I didn't dare to even mention Malcom X.

"Don't you know that now at least we are free to work where we want and when we want? Don't you all know that the days of washer ladies and step and fetch-its are over? Listen, I live in Orlando, which by the way is only 4-5 hours from here. I write for a BLACK newspaper and my husband is a minister that travels all over the country motivating blacks to be better, do better, and have better. Do you know what the NAACP is?"

At that remark he looked at me and said, "Chile', I say hush and listen. You still stupid an young and don't' know a thing 'bout de real world!'"

At that moment I felt as if I must have passed through some time continuum, or God was punishing me with a real glimpse of what being Black is really all about. And, it suddenly hit me that I was living in the year 2000.

He said he was born in 1820? And he was bragging on a 1920 Roadster Pickup. Something was definitely off, askew, downright not right and I was smack dab in the middle of it. Either way, I sat there hoping my cell phone would still dial the 11 digits I needed to make everything alright.

CHAPTER 2

I WOULDN'T LET A WOMAN IN MY PULPIT!

As I sat filled with indignation at this man's insults I was still intrigued by what lay ahead of me. Although I wanted to run to my car, jump in, drive away and never turn back, that seemed ironic. Never Turn Back. That's just what I had done and when I thought of the opportunities that I now held within my slim brown hands. I was filled with excitement.

Pastor Jonah Petersburg Limon sat looking at my face. I guess he was trying to tell just what emotions were running through my mind but since I had angrily put my sun glasses back on, he couldn't really get into my head. The eyes are the windows to the soul and I had effectively blocked him out!

He took my hand in his and said in a very quiet voice which made me have to lean towards him, "Chile, I ain't mean to hurt cha heart none. I just want you to be alright. Dis ain't, where you say you from? Oh! Yea, O'lando. By da way, where is O'lando? I ain't nevah heard tell of it an it seems kinda nice from what you say."

I just remained very still and quiet. It's hard for a feisty woman of the 21st century to get over hurt feelings.

"Well, I know you probably thirsty, huh?" he said patting my hand. It reminded me of the tender moments I spent with my grandfather in North Carolina, just him and me sharing some time and getting to know one another.

I turned to Pastor Jonah and in a small, quiet voice said, "No. I had plenty of juice on the drive here but thank you anyway. Tell me please, why is this called Limon County Parish?"

"Oh, now dat's an easy one. Ole' Cap'n Limon come back after de civil war' an bought up all dis land 'round here. He used to live in dat big ole house on de hill but now he's gone on to his final reward. He was a nasty ole man most times but den he had moments a kindness like when he gave me my house."

A smile crossed the old man's face and I wished for a camera to record this moment. Unfortunately, I'd not put that on my list of things to bring.

"Yea, de Ole' Cap'n came down one day while I's preaching de sermon a Jonah in de Whale's Belly. He sat down on a stump, well 'cause back den we ain't have no building we just met out in de open an praise de Lawd rain or shine. You do know dat story don't cha, chile? You did say you was a, what was dat name you called yo'self?"

"A Minister of the Gospel of Jesus Christ."

"Right! A minister. Dat sounds pretty good. Dey let women preach in yo' chuch do dey? Must not be Baptist 'cause I wouldn't let one git up in my pulpit."

There we go again! How many insults was I supposed to take from this man? Yes, respect your elders. Give every man his due. Do unto others and all that jazz but Pastor Jonah was coming dangerously close to seeing a little righteous indignation from Minister Yolanda! Oh! Don't think that I can't have a temper just because I'm a Minister, lest I start to remind you how many times Jesus rebuked and downright told off the scribes and Pharisees, and wreaked havoc in the synagogue.

"Well, Pastor Jonah, where I come from people are more open minded." Then I had to think about that statement. How many times had I had to fight for my rights not only as an African American, but as a woman?

"What I mean is, the word of God has many instances of women in the ministry and women helping out Jesus and the apostles. Who was it that found the tomb to be empty and get the message that the Messiah had risen while the men were in hiding? Mary— a woman. In my way of thinking, it doesn't matter who tells the truth and saves the souls as long as they are indeed saved."

Well, he had to think about that for a minute. While he was thinking I had time to walk over to my car and try to make a call on my cell phone. I desperately needed to speak with my husband, but as with all cell phones when you really need them, all circuits were busy!

I glimpsed my hand held recorder and decided to take it back over to Pastor Jonah's porch. When I sat down once again his eyes were riveted to my chest. No, he wasn't a pervert; he was trying to figure out what it said. I read it for him, "The Black Woman - Mother of the Earth." He just smiled and I suddenly noticed he was totally toothless and I just began to laugh. We laughed together, each for our own reasons, but nevertheless we laughed together.

We grew quiet and reflective for a while during which I did some quick math in my head. Pastor Jonah was born in 1820. Now, back in 1863 the slaves were supposedly set free. I say that because Lincoln himself was a believer in white supremacy and so the war initially was only fought to preserve the union.

However, he became more sympathetic to the idea after "Uncle Tom's Cabin", a book written by Harriet Beecher Stowe, was published and on September 22, 1862 issued a preliminary proclamation that wouldn't become effective until January 1, 1863 when slavery ended.

The Emancipation Proclamation didn't end slavery in and of itself, but rather the 13th Amendment to the Constitution on December 18, 1865, made that its basic war goal. General Lee surrendered at Appomattox on May 9, 1865 but the last of the confederate soldiers didn't surrender until late May of 1865. That would make Pastor Jonah 45 years old at that time.

The Jim Crow laws were in effect from 1880 until 1960. Slavery began in 1699 or maybe 1700. My memory was not that great but that means that Pastor Jonah was born during slavery and had not only to endure the bonds of slavery, but the Jim Crow laws as well. This meant that not only were his parents slaves, but he was too!

My God, what had I stumbled into? I was sitting next to a wealth of information on what slavery, Jim Crow and the entire struggle for African Americans had been like! Suddenly, my eyes grew large as I realized that it being the year 2000, Pastor Jonah had to be at least 180 years old and I almost passed out!

I clasped Pastor Jonah's hands in mine and asked if he would kindly tell me just a little about his life. This opportunity was getting better and better but at the same time stranger and stranger.

It was getting late in the afternoon and I wanted to hear just a little bit before I got back on the road. I didn't want to be driving along in these strange circumstances in the dark.

"Well, let me see. Not dat much ta tell. If you go down dis road 'bout, oh, 7 or 8 miles you can see de plantation I was born on. I was born to Mattie an Hezekiah Limon. My momma was de washer woman an I ain't git to see my daddy too much 'cause he sassed Ole' Cap'n Limon one to many times an was sold off. Dey say I look just like him tho' an dat's why de Ole' Cap'n ain't stand my company too much. I mostly worked 'round de stables an got pretty good at takin' care of de horses an animals in gen'ral."

"One day when I was 'bout 8, I was helping my momma take care of de clothes 'cause she was feeling po'ly. Ole' Cap'n came out back an ain't like it not one bit. He say ta me, "Nigga git yo' black hide back down ta dem stables an make sho' my horse is ready fo' me." Den he picked up a rock 'bout de size a my hand an thowed it at me. I tried ta duck outta de way but wasn't no help fo' it, dat rock hit me right in de middle a my forehead an I still got da mark."

He pointed to a mark that was oval shaped in his forehead and I reached out to feel it and when I touched his skin I felt the bone had caved in some. Tears started streaming down my face because I could feel the pain and I knew what it was like to get cracked in the head.

I asked if it bothered him any, and he just sniffed and told me, "Jus' a mite sometime, jus' a mite." As I wiped the tears away from my eyes, he caught a glimpse of a scar I had on my nose. He laughed, slapped his knee, and said, "Well, I guess you do know somethin 'bout being hit in de head."

It was getting on towards early evening and I needed to leave. I asked Pastor Jonah if it would be alright for me to come and visit his church next Sunday.

"I'd be proud ta have you come ta our lil' chuch. You 'memba where I said it was?"

"Yes sir, just down the road about 3 miles."

"Dat's right. Now we start chuch 'round 9 so you make sho' an be on time."

"I'd like to leave you something, Pastor Jonah, if you don't mind." I walked across to my car and pulled out my briefcase. Inside was a child's Sunday School book with pictures and easy words I thought he would be able to understand. I walked over and handed it to him. He looked down and saw the picture of David defeating the giant in battle. He asked a few questions and I answered.

"Well, I'll be going now. It has been such a pleasure sharing this time with you and I look forward to next Sunday." I smiled, kissed his forehead, said a silent prayer over him and walked over to my car. As I turned around in the road he waved at me and told me to be "mighty careful, it's gettin' dark." I smiled and assured him that God would take care of me.

On the ride back, I stopped at that same gas station just to make sure I had enough gas and the same attendant came out. He asked if I'd found what I was looking for and I exclaimed, "Yes!" with a huge smile. As I drove off he hollered, "See ya next Sunday!" I picked up my cell phone and called home.

Now you work, I thought, as my husband answered. "Honey, I'll be home soon and you better believe I have something to tell you about!"

CHAPTER
3

MY SOUL IS SATISFIED

Driving back on the next Sunday morning, I felt very at home and relaxed. Even though I had to leave Orlando around 4:30 in the morning I was happy. There I was going back to a place that seemed like home. Cruising in my Navigator listening to my Cd's and wondering what the church service would be like the drive didn't seem as long as the last time.

As I turned down Parish Road, I passed Pastor Jonah's house and felt a friendly and warm vibration in my heart. That old gentleman had touched my heart and I began to wonder about his life story. He certainly talked well for someone of his age and background, but then there had been educated slaves.

Just as he said, the little church was 3 miles down the road in a beautiful clearing. There were weeping willows all around, flower beds of azaleas and orchids, and there were even stumps that they used to sit on before they had the building. There seemed to be something peaceful about this spot. The sun's rays were falling down upon the clearing in such a way as to highlight the trees and stumps.

I was amazed when I saw the church building. I expected an old, run down building with some possible leaks in the roof. What graced my sight was a building that was loved and carefully tended to. It was freshly painted white, the doors were a brick red color and even the two steps leading to the doors were painted that color. Right outside of the front doors was two benches, one on either side and they were painted white and edged with flowers. Obviously, this was a church of love.

As I got out of my car I saw people staring at me. I just smiled, straightened my back, adjusted my Liz Claiborne suit (that I borrowed from my mother) and walked on inside. When I was a little girl, my father pastored a church in upstate New York - First Corinthians Baptist Church - and this church reminded me of it.

It brought back memories of the days we would go and clean the church before service. The times when my father would be in the pulpit and I would just run up and sit in his lap. The times when the testimony services would be going on and the young fry (me included) would just laugh at how they went on and on about God providing and taking care of them. Well, I certainly can understand that now because He has brought me through some scrapes.

But, the one part I remember most vividly was my brother's declaration. We were at the church, it seemed we spent more time there than at home. He looked at my mother and said, "You know what, when I grow up I'm gonna build me a church, go inside, say "AMEN!" and come back out!" My mother still laughs over that one.

They were starting devotional service and I didn't want to miss anything so I slipped in and sat on the back pew. The church felt so serene and peaceful. The people were kind of stand offish but I didn't take it to heart. I guess I looked like someone from outer space to them. As the deacons took their places, I said a silent prayer and asked God's blessing on this adventure in my life.

They began to sing songs like "A Charge To Keep I Have" or "Have You Got Good

Religion". When they began to sing "What a Friend We Have In Jesus" I just couldn't keep my seat because they sang it like they knew what a friend Jesus could be. Like it testified to all the times He saw them through and kept them whole and safe.

Finally, one of the oldest men I've ever seen came up to pray. His prayer was not eloquent but simple and from the heart. It went something like this:

"Dis mownin' our heav'nly Father we come ta say thank Ya. Thank Ya fo' wakin us up an thank Ya fo' bringing us here. We know dat widout Yo we could do nuthin' an so we jus' wanna tell Ya dat we love Ya 'cuz Ya first loved us. An now Father, be wid us an help us to un'erstan de word today an put it to use in our lives. We pray fo' de sick an de dying, de young, de old an de unsaved, an Lawd, we jus' thank Ya dis mownin fo saving our souls."

I found tears running down my eyes because in just a few words he had summed up how I felt. God had given me an opportunity to see what many couldn't see - how we got over... and I thanked Him.

As Pastor Jonah asked for the visitors to stand, I wasn't sure what to do. They would think me strange and I just wanted to fit in and identify with these people. So, when I ended up not standing he took a few minutes to introduce me to his congregation.

"Dis mornin' chuch,' he said in a very loud and authoritative voice, 'we have with us a friend a mine. She is a minister of de Gospel of Jesus Christ from O'lando an I'm glad dat she took de time dis day ta come an give thanks with us. My sistah, would you please stand?"

Trembling, I stood up and nodded my head to acknowledge everyone. They said, "Good Mownin," and I took my seat again.

There was no choir. People from the congregation just started out singing and everyone joined in and made such a joyful praise to the Lord that I knew He had to be smiling down upon us. Some of the songs, I had never heard but I caught on fast and began to enjoy this part of the service.

Most of the women wore white dresses and polished black shoes. The men had their very best suits or pants and shirt with shoes looking spit shined. They wanted to give their very best to the Lord and my heart jumped at this outpouring. Then, they had testimony service and the stories I heard of how the Holy Spirit had worked in their lives were amazing. There was one woman that got up to tell her testimony and it touched my soul.

"I been so sick de pass week an b'lieved I was goin' home ta meet my maker but what bother'd me de mos' was all de bills my family still owed on our land an widout my takin' in sewin' and washin' I knowed it would be hard fo' my babies to own de land. One night aftah ev'yone had gone ta bed, I declare I jus' couldn't take de pain no mo' an so I got up ta walk out into da woods ta die. While I's strugglin' an makin' my way, I begin talkin' ta my Lawd an tellin' Him what my wishes was fo' my family an de land we so dearly lubbed. I made it to my fav'rite spot an looked up at de moon an tole God, Well, I done struggle many a year an tried ta gibe my best. I raised my chulin de best I knowed how an now dey got chulin ta raise. I gibe what I owed de best I could an al'ays had some fo' chuch an now it my time. I'll just lie down here an wait fo' de chariot ta come on by an sweep me up ta meet ya. As I laid dere I begin to sing my fav'rite song - "My Soul Is Satisfied." As I was singing, I tell ya I felt a heat come in my body an 'mediately de pain begin to go 'way. I just kept on singing 'cuz I thought de Lawd was just preparin' me an de next thing I knowed, thar was a bright light in de sky. I felt someone standin' close by me. I kept layin' still an singin' my song 'cuz I just knowed dat my Jesus was sendin' de chariot soon fo' to carry me on home. Soon, I musta went off ta sleep singin' an when da chirpin' of de birds woke me de next mownin', all de pain was gone an I got right on up an started thanking da Lawd 'cuz I knowed he done sabed me to libe an fight on fo' my family."

The whole service was wonderful and the preaching, of course, was inspiring. Pastor Jonah taught on the boy who slew the giant and everyone loved it. I noticed that he didn't carry a bible and I didn't see any in the church.

As the service came to an end, and people were greeting one another, that same lady with the testimony came over to me and invited me to eat. I thought about all of her children and said that I just couldn't.

She told me that every Sunday Pastor Jonah came to her house to eat and since I was his guest that's what I was going to do, too. I learned her name then, Martha Mary Petersburg. She was such a sweet woman and I just reached down and gave her the biggest hug.

When the Pastor came out and closed up the church, I said that I would follow them in my car. He looked at me, shook his head and said, "Well, I guess dey ain't make dem shoes fo' walkin'." I laughed and offered them a ride, which they gladly took.

As I opened the door to my car, they looked as if they didn't want to get in. I asked, rather timidly, what was wrong and they said it looked so clean and they had never seen carpet in a car. I laughed and told them to get right on in and enjoy the ride.

I forgot that I had my music turned up, so when I turned on the car - John P. Kee started singing his heart out. They covered their ears and I immediately turned off the Cd. The Pastor was looking at everything and trying to be inconspicuous but I saw his eyes and hands touching things.

I told him that I loved the message and then I asked him why he didn't carry a bible. He said that the Lord hadn't provided him with one yet. In actuality, only white folks had access to bibles and he was just being polite.

I turned off onto another dirt road and kept following directions. Martha Mary lived in a tiny little house with a field of corn and other vegetables on one side and just some dirt for the babies to play in on the other side. In the back of the house was the outhouse and an old willow tree blowing in the wind next to the clothes line.

When we pulled up the grandchildren, who had already made it home from service, saw her getting out of the car and came running out of the door full of curiosity and excitement. At first they just stood nervously hopping from one foot to the other but when they saw my warm smile and bright eyes they ran over and asked to see "it".

I was introduced to Martha's 8 children and her 5 grandchildren. They were all so plain yet elegant in their movements and manners. Not like back in Orlando where a child of 5 would curse you out first and then shoot you with his 9MM.

One of the children, a beautiful little girl with dark skin, big brown eyes, two thick braids hanging down her back and the sweetest smile I'd ever seen took my hand and looked up at me with a grin.

I looked down at her and asked her name.

"Talitha... I 8 years ole'. I like you." She ducked her head down with a laugh and I immediately lost my heart to her.

She didn't look 8 years old; she was a small child that I thought to be around 5 years old.

I would later find out from her mother that Talitha was born 3 months early and at birth was only 2 pounds. Right after the birth her heart had stopped beating and it was only the quick thinking of her grandmother, Martha Mary that saved her little life.

She bounced back quickly and after 6 months of being cared for around the clock by Martha Mary she was eating and growing. She was slow in speaking, small of stature, and mostly stayed to herself. And the family was amazed with her taking to me and talking to me so fast.

I reached down and picked her up and once she was in my arms I gave her a big kiss and told her that she and I were going to be the best of friends.

Upon entering the house, I found that it had only four rooms and held 16 occupants. Now, I know that I would not be able to handle that because I got myself in an uproar when we used to have company in our large family home. Looking around, I began to see the character of this family.

In the main room of the house which served as the kitchen, living room, dining room, family area, bathing area, and Martha Mary's sewing room, I saw 5 rocking chairs with seat cushions that were worn but not tattered.

There was a large woven rug that covered a good part of the wood floor and a table with only 4 chairs next to the stove. The stove was an old cast iron one with the lids you had to lift in order to stoke the fire and the stove pipe went out through a hole in the roof. There was also a crudely made sink with a brown cloth around the edge to make the contents underneath invisible to guests.

Off in one corner was the area used for Martha Mary's sewing. In another corner, a sheet hanging from the ceiling helped to hide the bathing area which was only a large tin tub and a place for soap.

But on the walls of this room were pictures. Beautiful, hand drawn pictures depicting the life of Jesus, the woman at the well, David and Goliath, John the Baptist preaching in the wilderness and many others. It gave the room such a peaceful air, a divine solitude, a warmth that permeated your very heart. I didn't see the other rooms but I can tell you that if they were anything like that one, they were exquisitely decorated.

The daughters of Martha Mary were all very shy but polite. Their names were, yes you guessed it, biblical. There was Sarah, Ruth, Esther, Rachel and Mary. The boys' names were Solomon, David, and Stephen.

They were all going about getting the food to the table and making sure that the Pastor and I were comfortable. I spent most of my time before dinner holding and talking with little Talitha. She was such a delight and very bright indeed once you got her to talk with you.

When dinner was finally ready, we all went out back. There in the backyard underneath the willow tree was a long table. The table was covered with a white tablecloth and there was a fresh bouquet of dandelions in the middle of it. Overhead the birds were chirping and the sun was shining brightly.

We were seated with Pastor Jonah at the head of the table and we bowed our heads as he blessed the food. Once the blessing was said, we all dug in. My stomach had been growling and upon seeing all the delicious food that was on that table, I realized I was truly famished.

There was a lightly glazed ham with the juices still running down the side, a basket full of homemade biscuits so fluffy and golden they looked as if they would float off the table, the most delicious corn with the butter sliding down the sides, hand-picked green beans, wonderful smelling candied yams and some down home potato salad.

Dessert was to be pound cake with strawberries and cream. The aroma of all these delectable foods floated through the air and into my nostrils causing my mouth to water. As the dishes were passed around, I gave one fleeting thought to my waistline and then indulged my taste buds.

After dinner, we all sat around the table and talked. The children played in the yard and their laughter echoed out and rang in my ears. During the conversation, I asked who was responsible for all those life-like bible images that hung on the wall of the house. Proudly, Ruth spoke up. "My sweet lil' girl done those."

I looked at her a moment and then asked, "Do you mean Talitha?"

She grinned and replied, "Oh! Yes. My baby jus' sat down one day and drew them pictures. She always been one for the bible and so she drew what she had heard 'bout. We, none of us, could hardly believe it but I hung 'em on the wall. It's the best part of her. Love." As she finished up her eyes glazed over and she lapsed into silence.

"Well' I said, "They are beautiful and she has a wonderful gift. They are very life-like and they capture your thoughts." I couldn't believe that this little child who everyone believed to be slow was exhibiting this kind of creativity. It was truly a gift from God and it needed to be nurtured.

Long after I had departed from that little house, I could still hear the children laughing and calling out to each other. And, in my mind I still saw little Talitha waving to me as I drove away from the house. Who would have thought that such joy and contentment could reside in that little house of Martha Mary's?

I gave Pastor Jonah a ride to his house. On the way there we talked about the family and how blessed they really were. I shared with him that where I came from most people don't believe you can be happy unless you have a big house, brand new car and money in the bank. Somehow, comparing those children with the ones I knew made me understand that simplicity really is a treasure.

As I pulled up to Pastor Jonah's house, he hesitated before opening the car door. He turned to me and asked if I would like to come next Sunday and speak at the Annual Women's Day Celebration. Well, as you can imagine, I was taken aback but I quickly accepted. He got out of the car and asked me to make sure that I was wearing red and white and to please speak about faith. Absentmindedly I said yes and when he closed the door I pulled away with a wave of my hand.

My mind was still wrapped around that little house and my new friend, Talitha. Her name was fitting given her story and I intended to be a wonderful friend and mentor to her. I wondered if her mother would mind me spending time with her, teaching her and nurturing her gift. I had no children of my own and somehow this little girl filled a void in me.

As usual, I stopped at the little gas station on the way out. The attendant that came to the car was different from last time but very friendly. He filled my tank and I told him not to bother checking the oil. Before I pulled off he said to me, "Guess you'll be back next Sunday. This place is really a part of you, don't you know." Then he walked back into the station.

As I drove off, my mind debated with him but I was tired and began to let the music take me away. Riding down the road, I began to sing "My Soul Is Satisfied" because truly this was one Sunday that the message came through loud and clear and I was totally and completely satisfied.

CHAPTER
4

COME THIS FAR BY FAITH

That very next Sunday found me heading back to Limon County Parish. I was so excited because Pastor Jonah had asked me to teach a lesson on the importance of faith. First of all, I recognized this as an honor because as I had learned earlier, he didn't let no woman in his pulpit! Maybe I'd impressed him as someone with a good heart or maybe he thought it was a good idea since it was the Annual Women's Day Celebration. Then again, maybe he just wanted to see how his people would receive me— and that thought made me very nervous.

Although I had only been in this church one time and the Pastor had introduced me as his guest, I wasn't sure how they would take to a woman outside of their community trying to speak on behalf of God.

By the time I reached the little church and parked, I was sweating and fully convinced that this day would be one that I would list in my "screamers" chapter. Nevertheless, I would do what I had been asked to do.

On this particular Sunday, all of the women were to wear red and white so I was dressed accordingly. I decided upon a long, red Donna Karan skirt with a 5 inch split that went from the ankles up and a white cotton blouse that had long sleeves and oversized cuffs.

As I disembarked from the Navigator, I pulled out my bible and another study book that I would use during my message. I also took 2 gift wrapped packages from the back seat. These I would give at the end of my message.

When I entered the church I was pleasantly surprised. The church had been decorated for the day and it was absolutely gorgeous. There were red and white carnations surrounding the pulpit area and each bench sported a red or white bow. The front rows were reserved for the women of the church and they were covered with white linen.

Most of the women were standing outside of the church because on this special day, they were given the honor of marching in and singing whatever song they had decided upon as the theme for their day. For today, it was "We Have Come This Far by Faith." I was instructed to go put my things in the pulpit then come back and, along with Martha Mary, lead the women into the church singing. I was honored.

The service began and the deacons said a prayer and then asked everyone (the men and children) to stand to honor the "Sisters" of the church. When everyone had stood, Martha Mary looked at me and said, "Well, start us."

So, I took a deep breath and in my soprano voice began to sing. "We have come this far by faith. Leaning on the Lord. Trusting in His holy word. He's never failed me yet. Singing, Oh ~ ~. Can't turn around. We've come this far by faith." My heart was pounding but I was so happy to be a part of this.

As I thought about it, the women that I was standing with had surely come a long way, bearing their burdens in the heat of the day and knowing that the Lord would see them through and make a way. Losing babies to the selling block, disease, poor nutrition and knowing that only their prayers could possibly save them. Having to submit their bodies to the whim of a master and seeing the hurt in their husband's eyes as the door closed in his face. Raising and sometimes breast feeding the master's children only to have them grow up and have to call them master or mistress and submit to them. Knowing that at any time a wrong deed, misunderstood word, and slow action could have them beaten or sold away from their family.

Sweet Lord, would I have made it through that long journey? Did I have the strength that these women had? Should I be speaking to them or listening to them speak to me?

Once inside the church, I continued on up to the pulpit and as I turned to watch the other women, such a feeling of belonging came over me. They were my sisters. Anyone of them could have been my grandmother, mother, or maybe an aunt. Just watching them hold their heads high and march with such purpose and determination gave me courage.

There was one woman who looked to be in her mid-forties in a starched and ironed white cotton blouse and red skirt. Her clothes were worn but clean. Her black leather shoes were worn and runned down but she stepped lively and with such self-respect.

Another Sister that appeared to be around 80 years old was coming down the aisle in-between her daughter and granddaughter. She was determined and proud and only allowed them to hold her elbows. Every step she took was labored and beads of sweat broke out on her forehead, but she made it all the way to the very first bench and stood there leaning on her cane.

The lines of age and worry shown in her face and the callouses from hard labor were on her hands. I saw very clearly the whelps that had formed around her neck and that probably extended the length of her shoulders and back. Nevertheless, pride illuminated from her eyes and the way she held her shoulders. This was a woman that had lived a harsh life but never, if she could help herself, asked for help from anyone.

When they reached the front benches, they stood and continued singing. They moved from song to song with ease and the harmony would have put some of the best choirs to shame. Some sang with their eyes closed and heads tilted upwards as if telling God...this is just for You. Some sang with heads straight forward, eyes uplifted, and hands clasped in front of their chest as if they were truly enraptured. Others held onto one another and sometimes when the words fit they looked into each others eyes and smiled a knowing smile as if to say...you and me Sister, we made it over. All the while they were singing the Lord was speaking to my heart and rewriting the message I was to give.

When we finished that segment of the service, Pastor Jonah stepped forward and began to talk about the day and its significance. "Brothas and Sistahs, today we come here to celebrate the gift from Gawd called woman. Her strength, 'termination, will, and beauty. When Gawd made her, he said she would be a helpmate and he was right. When Gawd made her, he gave her a heart for us men folk and the chil'ren. When Gawd made her, he knew dat every home would need one to keep it going and to keep it thinkin' on him. Wives, Mothas, Sistahs, Anties.... we thank the Masta for them and come dis day to celebrate them."

When he finished speaking, he held up his hands and the children came forward to sing a song for the women. Some of the little ones were squirming and pulling at their clothes but once they started to sing, "Jesus..Thank

You for Her" they stopped and concentrated on the song. "Jesus made a woman, her name was called Eve. She is the mother of this earth, a blessing Adam did receive. Now that she's in heaven, we have to only look around. For she left us others right here, let us make a joyful sound. Thank You for her, my mother and sister. Thank You for her, my auntie too. God knew just what He was doing, when He made them. Thank You for her dear Lord, For each and every one of them."

I'm sure the smile on my face was a wide one because you can just imagine the mispronounced words, the late words and those just making noise. But you can surely also imagine the heartfelt sincerity coming from these little hearts. When they finished they all rushed over to the women and gave them hugs and kisses. How wonderful to be a child and act without reservation.

Once again, Pastor Jonah stood and this time he was introducing me. I really hadn't told him that much about myself but he seemed to know just what the important things to say were.

"Dis mornin' chuch, I have de pleasure of bringin' you one who de Lawd has touched. She is young but loves the Lawd. She is from O'lando and today will give us de word from on high. Open your minds and hearts to her for truly I know dat de good Lawd dwells in her heart. Brothas and Sistahs, Minister Yolanda."

There was no clapping, there was no patting of feet, but an air of acceptance and expectancy greeted me when I stood before this congregation. I didn't reach for my bible nor did I want my other book. The simple message was burning within my heart and I was eager to tell it!

"Brothers and sisters, I thank Pastor Jonah for opening up his pulpit to me and having the faith to know that I'm a messenger of God. You all have made me feel so welcome and a part of this community. It is truly a pleasure and an honor to be here with you today.'

This day has been dedicated to the women of this community. As I look at them, I see the strength, the honor, the sheer magnificence of their womanhood. Wives, mothers, daughters, sisters, and aunts. Struggling together for their families, striving for the advancement of their community, and wholly leaning on the powerful arms of our loving Father.'

I could talk to you about Ruth and her devotion to her mother-in-law Naomi and how she was determined to be a credit to her and a blessing."

"Yes!" exclaimed Pastor Jonah.

"I could go into the story of Esther and her obedience to her Uncle Mordecai and how through that and her willingness to yield herself as a vessel to God, she saved her people."

"Amen!" shouted Pastor Jonah again.

"I could also tell you about Rahab the harlot who yielded herself to the leading of the Master and opened up her home and hid the Israelite spies and helped them to escape and as a result of that her house was saved from bloodshed."

"Well!" I heard someone else shout.

"But, what lies within in my heart is closer than those stories; it's not centuries behind us but right here with us! You don't have to look back to see it and you don't have to reach ahead to grab a hold of it because you have shining examples of what a woman surrendered to God is within your very midst."

I went on from there to tell about the virtues I saw in the women, their dependence upon God and their willingness to let Him lead them no matter where it took them. As I finished up, I began to quote Proverbs 31 and as I did, I would point out certain women in the congregation and they would stand to their feet.

Tears were streaming down my face because I realized that this was probably the best message I'd ever give and I was thanking God for using me to uplift these worthy women. When I ended my message, I stepped down from the pulpit and began to sing a song that my mother and I used to sing together. "I've had many tears and sorrows; I've had questions for tomorrow. There've been times I've felt so all alone. Yet in my lonely hours. Yes, those precious lonely hours. God let me know that I was His own. Through it all. O! Through it all. I've learned to trust in Jesus. I've learned to trust in God. Through it all. O! Through it all. I've learned to depend upon His word."

As I sang, the women began to cry because it seemed that I was singing to the heart of what had kept them. Faith, trust, hope and learning to depend upon the Master. Knowing what the world was showing you but trusting in what the Lord had promised you. Seeing the many trials and tribulations but choosing to believe in what God had promised you must come. Cradling dying loved ones in your arms, knowing that your face was the last they would see; your voice was the last they would hear. Choosing to give them words of encouragement from God. Whosoever believes in me shall not perish but have life everlasting.

Holding your man back from going to the master and committing an act that would surely bring death all the while choosing to use not words of affection from your heart but God's word. Vengeance is mine saith the Lord.

Trying your best to raise your children to be respectful, productive, and worthy human beings. When they make mistakes, chastising them with the rod but also with words of correction and not your own but God's words. Children obey your parents for this is right in the Lord. Honor thy father and mother.

All of these thoughts were in the minds of the virtuous women and I thanked God that I could be the one to tell them that their struggles had not been in vain. Their lives would not go unheralded. Their legacies would live on and their footsteps would be followed.

I thanked God for this opportunity to show me the heart of the washer women that so many have made fun of; the purpose of the old mammies that I've read about; the soul of the cotton picker, the field worker and the woman set to breeding.

There are times that only God can show the real deal about things on this earth and those are the times when the message hits home and you take stock of yourself.

As I finished my song, I went to each woman and hugged her with love and admiration. I wanted them to know that I counted it an honor to be in their presence and to be a part of this lovely occasion.

CHAPTER
5

A HURT SO DEEP-ROOTED IT CAN'T COME OUT

The men had planned a picnic for the church on this day and so, after service was concluded and we were dismissed with the peace of God upon us, we adjourned to the open space behind the church building.

The beauty of this land was indescribable. There was plush, carpet-like grass that was so green I felt that if I sat on it, it would permanently stain my clothes. The trees were tall and so large that it would take ten people to circle around it holding hands. The leaves were large and droopy. These were the places where tables were set because of the great amount of shade from the sun afforded by the trees. Of course, I just had to walk over and sit on one of the stumps that they used prior to having the building.

Just sitting in that clearing gave me such a lift in my soul that I didn't want to move. I closed my eyes and lifted my face up towards heaven and began to commune with God. I'd never felt such a closeness, such a pure sense of His presence as I did at that very moment.

I began to pray and as I did I remembered everything that I'd ever wanted to ask God for or about and these prayers were sent up to Him silently. Tears had begun to slide down my face by the time I was ending my prayer and the last words uttered from my lips were these— "Father, may I always remember this moment when You were so very close to my heart and I knew that all was well with my soul."

As, I opened my eyes, I was surprised to see the sisters from the church encircling me. They had been standing there all along and praying right along with me. I brushed the tears from my cheeks and looked into the eyes of the 80 year old woman who stood smiling down upon me. She opened her arms and I gratefully stepped into her embrace. I could hear her whispering a prayer over me. I hugged each woman and they all whispered prayers over me and I felt as though I were going through some sort of initiation into a group.

When I had hugged the last woman, we all took our seat on the stumps and began to talk. In the background, the men were barbecuing in an open pit and the children were playing down by the creek that ran in the back of the church.

I had so many questions to ask but I didn't want to seem too eager or too nosy. I wanted to know what their lives had been like. Had they all been slaves or had some been born free? Was this the only home they'd ever known?

Finally, one lady said to me, "Suga', we know you got thangs to axe us. Go on 'head. We don't min' none at all." So, I turned to the oldest woman in the group, the 80 year old Sister with the cane, and asked her where she had been born and if it was during slavery.

She puckered her lips and looked at me for a moment. "Baby, I was bon' durin' slabry an ain't n'ber knowed no other place but Limon Parish. Dey say, de night I's bon it was cold and rainy an de midwife had to keep turnin' me roun' cause I didn't wanna come out. Guess I's nice and warm inside Mammy. Mammy had it hard. I come out feet furst and liked to kill my po' mammy. She mos' died wid giving birth to me but de good Lawd pull her on through dat. The cabin I's bon in used ta be right down yonda by de creek but it gone now.'

"When I's raised, not by Mammy 'cause ole' Massa Limon say I's ta be his daughter play girl, I was gibed food right from de kitchen and got to sleep in de big house at de foot a Missy's bed. She was nice 'nough but I wanted ta be wit Mammy. Sometime at night, when de moon shinin' real bright and up real high, me an' Mammy sneak out behind de barn. We sit an' talk for hours sometime, cuz you know once white people sleep dey don' wake up hardly none. Mammy tell me 'bout who was my Pappy.'

"She say dey sold her man 'way after he tried ta tell Massa Limon his horse wan't good 'nough ta make de trip ta sell. It wan't no lie but he's lookin' Massa right in de eye and dat what got him whip and sold way. Mammy telled me dat after dat Massa took to comin' ta her at night. Dat how I get here. Yes, Lawd, I'm one a Massa babies jus' like a whole heap others are. She say he promise neber ta sell me and dat good 'nough for her.'

"One day when I's 12 or so, dey done 'cide ta sell my Mammy way cause she old and can't hep no more. I got spittin' mad an went ta Missy. She tell me to go on an fetch her bath water an stay out white folks biznes. Humph! I fetched her water an put so much lye in it when she put her foot in she scream fo dear life! Ev'yone come a runnin' an I's jus standin' in de corner hummin' ta myself wishin' Missy had jump in head furst! Dat how I got des marks on my back. Dey whip me so long I pass out and even after all dat, I neber get ta see my Mammy agin."

She got quiet and the tears streaming down her face showed her hurt still ran deep. I guess that's what slavery did more than anything else. Produce a hurt so deep and so rooted that it can't be cut out and it can't be loved out; it can only be covered over and hoped that something beautiful grows on top of it to keep its ugliness buried.

As I drove back home that night, I reflected upon the stories the women told. Some had been sold from place to place and finally freedom found them in Limon Parish, with families and no jobs to speak of but a peace and contentment in their souls. No longer would they be on the auction block. No more could they come from the fields to find their babies gone, sold away from them. No more midnight visits from the master of the plantation or even the guests he invited into his home.

The stories were poignant and they were so heart wrenching but the truth from them rang so clear. They had survived what many, including myself, could never have come through.

They were the women we all longed to be. Strong, determined, able, wise, and most of all still standing after they had taken what could only be described as "the best shot" humanity had to offer.

Thank you, Jesus! Thank You for the mammies. Thank You for the field hands. Thank You for the breeders. Thank you for those who came before me and blazed a trail of "Can Do" instead "Give In".

CHAPTER
6

WHAT'S THE DEAL, THIS IS THE 21ST CENTURY

When I arrived back in Orlando that night, I tossed my keys and things on the hall table and called out to my husband. There was no answer. I went into the living room to see if he had fallen asleep on the sofa watching his favorite news broadcast but it was empty. I tiptoed into the bedroom and found the bed made and only a note for me resting on my bedside table. I picked it up only to read that he had been called away on a family emergency and that he would call me in the morning.

I knew that he had to be worried about the trips I was taking and thus had made up my mind to tell him just what was going on. Maybe, it was all in my head. I thought that if I laid down on the bed and concentrated hard enough it would come to me just what was going on here. Why would I be experiencing such a wealth of information? Why me?

Purely by habit, I grabbed the remote and flicked on the television set. There was the face. The familiar face of a man that meant trouble was brewing in the African American community and he was there to forewarn and foretell of the impending disaster to the establishment if nothing changed.

"We are tired," he was saying. "Tired of being low men and women on the totem pole. When will America recognize our contribution and our value and give us that which is no more than our right as American citizens! I tell you, it's going to rain people! Not that physical rain you can run and duck under an umbrella from, not that physical rain that flood, but rain destruction. The type of which this country has never known, the type of which this establishment cannot afford to let happen. For this rain will be destructive, unproductive and hard to outlive if nothing is done. We deserve equal rights under the law, we deserve equal rights in pay and job., We deserve equal rights!'"

Oh! "My God!" I uttered as I sat up in the bed. What is going on? Who has been killed? What little child has been denied? What teenager has been shot unjustly? What? What is going on in this country now?

I watched further as he walked determinedly away from the lectern and another familiar face filled the screen.

"Today, we will not delay. We will not hesitate to take action, for the time has come for satisfaction. Don't try to cover us under paperwork because that would be an insult. Don't try to make this go away for destruction will be the result. Listen, and listen good for the trouble is not only in our 'hood. Soon, you too will be the object of this fascination and then to whom will you turn in this nation. No, we won't be denied that which is ours for the time has come to turn on our power. To the establishment we say with dismay, don't look away, and don't try in your comfort zones to stay. We are coming out in full force and you will deal with us or destruction will be the main course!"

What? What did I miss? Hurriedly, I turned to CNN hoping to catch some glimpse of what had provoked this action, this call to arms for that is most certainly what it was. Just as I was about to despair, the telephone rang.

"Hello, Honey. I see you finally made it back home." I was only too glad to hear his voice and I couldn't stop myself from smiling. Then I remembered. "Sweetie, what is going on? Why are they on television issuing declarations and talking about a coming destruction?" There was silence on the line and then he answered me with a tone of voice that said, "You really are out of touch."

"Honey, today in Celebration a young black man was shot to death by the police. They aren't sure exactly what he was doing in Celebration because he didn't live there. But the scoop is they thought he was casing the homes so that later he and his gang could come back and collect. The problem... he was an honor roll student, an All American Football player named in Who's Who, headed to University of Florida under full scholarship, and on top of that has NEVER had any trouble with the law. Not even a speeding ticket. They found no weapon on him, no drugs. Only $30.00 and a pack of

Juicy Fruit. It's going to get ugly around here and I want you to stay close to home."

Close to home? Was he kidding? I was onto something and I would not just let it go. "I promise to be careful, but you know I have to find out what's going on with this. I don't just sit around and twiddle my thumbs when these two get upset. When will you be home?"

"Probably on Friday. Everything here is going well and my sister is feeling much better now. Honey, I love you... and be careful."

"I love you, Sweetie and I promise to be careful." We hung up and I turned off the television and went directly to my computer. This was going to be big and I wanted to be in the know.

What I found on the information highway was nothing more than the usual drivel and it made me even more determined and upset. What was the deal? We're living in the 21st

Century and police don't just shoot people for not good reason, or do they? NO! Come on! What's going on? I sent an email to a friend in D.C. and then decided to call it a night. There would be time enough tomorrow to learn the details and get involved.

CHAPTER
7

IF YOU'RE ON YOUR KNEES, YOU'D BETTER BE PRAYING!

The next Sunday found me heading back to Limon Parish County. I was on a mission this time so I didn't even bother to dress for church because I knew by the time I arrived they would be at home eating. On the seat beside me, I had my usual tape recorder and pad and pen. But, I had with me this time a package of information about the youth that had been shot in Celebration.

I had that Saturday attended his funeral and I can only tell you that it was full of emotion and the tide of destruction was rising. At the services the church was overflowing with people. Young and old, people from every spectrum of life who wanted to come and show their respects.

The two policemen that were responsible for this tragedy were on suspension and currently "unavailable" to anyone. The eulogy pointed out that we must, as a race, come together. It was time for us to be a nation, a people undivided and stand together in order to stop this senseless tide of stereotypical action.

"When God when?' and, 'Why God why?" were the questions of the day and no one had answers. There was to be a press conference that following Thursday to try and guide the tide that was swelling.

I spoke briefly with the mother of the deceased teenager and tried to reassure her that she was not alone. I tried to let her know that her Father above was right there with His loving arms around her bearing her and her burden up. She was distraught and could barely notice that someone was talking to her. Finally, I just hugged her and, as my sisters had done in that clearing behind the church, whispered a prayer over her.

When I reached Limon County Parish, as usual, Pastor Jonah Petersburg Limon was sitting on his porch. But, this time he had a look of resolution in his face. He was holding a book in his hands that was worn and tattered.

I parked in front of his house, gathered my things and walked up the path that leads to his gate. As I approached, he looked up and gave me one of those toothless smiles that only Pastor Jonah could give. I took a seat next to him and we just sat quietly for a while. I reached over for his hand and held it hoping to find that steadying calmness he so often had given me.

After a while, I spoke to him. "Good afternoon, Pastor Jonah. I'm sorry I missed service today but I was just too tired to make the early morning trip. I attended a very emotional funeral yesterday and I'm so worried. Have you ever just been worried in your soul? Not your mind so much but your soul? Way down deep where it's hard to get to and examine the whole matter?"

He rocked for a minute and then he answered in a solemn voice. "Chile, I been worried down deep for years but I jus' don' talk ta no one 'bout it. Sometimes you gotta reach inside and catch hold of that faith that's been planted. It 'bout the only thing that can see ya through tragedy and turmoil. You say the fun'ral was 'motional? Someone you knew?"

I shifted in my seat and tried to relate as best I could just what I was feeling. "Pastor

Jonah, there was a young boy, a good boy, that was shot and killed for no apparent reason. He was just somewhere they didn't want him to be. He had good grades and was headed for a great future but now, nothing. No college, no family life, no success. Nothing but coldness and darkness where there was light and warmth of a future well planned."

I fumbled in my lap and produced the newspaper article with a picture of the boy on it.

"Do you see? Look at that young face full of life and ambition. Now, the whole African American nation is up in arms because once again for no good reason, no reason at all, one of our young hopes for the future has been eliminated. Why can't we just learn to let people live and be free? Do you know that two of our most respected leaders are calling for us to totally become a nation unto ourselves? They want us to pull out of all establishments that are owned, operated, or affiliated with anyone of a different race. And for once, we are all on one accord. It reminds me of the people building the tower of Babel in the bible. We are all on one accord and that scares me because when people are of one mind and one purpose what they can accomplish is awesome."

I hadn't noticed Pastor Jonah staring at the boy's picture. He was looking with an expression of sheer awe and bewilderment. His hands were clutching the brown tattered book and he was shaking violently. "This young man's name was Jonah Petersburg?"

I looked at him and then at the picture, the resemblance was uncanny. The same nose, the same jaw set, the same forehead, that line of determination that ran from the temples.

"Why, yes Pastor Jonah. That was his name. He was born and raised right here in Florida. As a matter of fact, according to my research, he was born in Pensacola but later his family moved to Orlando. My Lord, the resemblance is tremendous! He could be your grandson!'"

That is when the whole purpose of this time became clear to me. That is when I knew I had been granted this opportunity for a greater cause, something greater than just my experience and knowledge, a greater cause than self. This was something that had been allowed for the greater advancement of not just my race, but my nation.

CHAPTER
8

NO LONGER STAND UP
NOT TO BE COUNTED

Thursday morning was cold, rainy, and filled with an air of expectancy. I had planned on rising early enough to enjoy some morning herbal tea with lightly buttered toast. I usually did so while sitting in my special chair in my "private" room. But, when the body is tired you can only ask for so much cooperation.

So, I found myself jumping out of bed with only an hour to get dressed and arrive at the fairgrounds in Orlando. As I shot past my husband's picture on the hall table, I stopped for a moment to whisper. "I sure wish you were here with me today, baby. I need you."

When I arrived at the Fairgrounds, I could see that this was going to be a day to be remembered. The people were crowding into the seats and some were already making little sitting areas on the cold ground. Umbrellas were opened, children were still bleary eyed, and the adults were stern faced.

For the number of people already assembled, the quiet was astonishing. The one thing that registered in my brain was that every person there, as far as I could see, was wearing a red tee shirt, black jeans, and a green arm band.

As I walked through the crowd, I could sense the determination that no longer would they stand up and not be counted, no more loud talk without meaning but there would be intelligent talk loaded with ear shattering action. I sensed the people had reached down within themselves and pulled out their inherited fortitude and strength of character.

Some held tightly to pictures of loved ones. I could only assume that these had either passed on through questionable violence or they were ancestors here to lend a voice if only through a tattered image. Some clung to old, weathered Bibles. Others clung to each other.

There was a group that stood just off to the side of the main stage and they were talking furiously among themselves. As I approached that side of the stage to make my way back to the area of preparation, they began to sing in the most melodic tones. Those tones that soothed the soul yet stirred it to remember and motivated it to action. They were singing, "I don't feel no ways tired. Come too far from where I started from. Nobody told me the road would be easy. I don't believe He brought me this far to leave me."

For just a moment, I was paralyzed. The song was ministering to me. The words hit a chord in my soul. I couldn't move my feet. All I could do was stand with my eyes closed as I felt the warmth growing in my heart. I wanted to reach up to heaven and tell God, "Please Master, right now just hold me. Let me feel Your loving embrace if only for a second. Then, I know that my strength will be made perfect through You despite my weakness."

When I entered the room where those who would be a part of the program were being housed, the noise was deafening. The immense difference between "the people" and those who were speaking to and for "the people" was tremendous.

Just inside the door, I stopped. Amazed and appalled. Were these the people who were demanding we all wear the symbolic colors yet only two or three were in them? Could these be the ones that said to us this rally would be non-violent, orderly, peaceful and full of intelligent power yet they were arguing among themselves? No, No! God this cannot— this shall not be!

As soon as I gathered myself, I walked over to the two brothers that were dressed symbolically and grabbed them by the hands. They looked up questioningly and then as if some communication had taken place they stood with me. We stood silent and united. We stood calm in the storm. We stood– and I started praying– out loud.

"Heavenly Father, first let us come to You and praise You for giving us another day. Another day in which we can be Your representatives, Your voice and Your vessels. Father we thank You for Your mercy, Your grace and Your unconditional love. But, most of all we want to thank You for thinking enough of us to impart Your wisdom to us for use in this great moment. For our intent is not to divide but to unify. Our purpose is not to bring anger and pain, but rather joy and peace through sharing the vision You have imparted to us. Now, Father as we go forth be with us. Let Your love operate fully in our hearts and minds to do as You have called us to do. Let no division have dominion; let not evil in among us. For we call to us peace, joy, love, fulfillment, wisdom and the spirit of unity. Bless us that we may bless others. Teach us that we may teach others. Guide us that we may guide others. Lord, prepare us to be Your sanctuaries. Fit for Your use and filled with Your divine love. Amen."

As I finished my prayer I held tightly to the hands of my two brothers. Tears were streaming down my face and I wanted to hold onto the peace that had come in to be with us. I guess everyone else needed that also, because we just stood. Holding hands, unmoving, silent. We stood. Peacefully affirming our mission. We stood. Together.

CHAPTER
9

CHAPTER

TALITHA'S SEED

As I passed the article and the funeral program to Pastor Jonah his facial expression went from one of sheer bewilderment to one of recognition and acknowledgment. He read the funeral obituary very carefully and then with a frail, thin finger pointed to a name on the program. In the section that listed the family there was a name that rang out clear as a bell... "Talitha Limon Petersburg."

I stared and tried to put it all together but my mind was not working right due to lack of sleep. Talitha Limon Petersburg? Who is that? What is she to Pastor Jonah? I looked at him with questioning eyes and he sat back in his chair and with a sigh began to weave a story for me.

"Chile, I b'lieve I can put this clear in yo mind. Let me see, now. You 'member little Talitha, Martha Mary's granddaughter that you met?' I shook my head yes. "Well, she in the family way you know."

No, I didn't know and was quite surprised to hear the news. She was so young but then we were talking about a place that time had forgotten.

Pastor Jonah continued. "She having a baby fo my grandson, he be called after me - Jonah Petersburg. You may 'member him from chuch. The quiet one wit de limp. He in his early twenties but you can't tell 'cause he slow. Them two took a likin' time they saw each other. They s'pose to marry soon."

My expression must have been one of horror because Pastor Jonah just took my hand and squeezed it really tight. I could not imagine the enormity of what was being revealed. I just sat with my hand clinging desperately to his, sweat forming on my forehead, and the early signs of what promised to be a dozy of a headache.

My God! Just what had I stumbled into...did I stumble or was I led by some unseen hand....and how was I ever going to relay this extraordinary experience to a nation full of mistrustful, fearful, head strong people. If I ever needed the Lord, I surely needed Him right now.

CHAPTER
10

JONAH'S ROCKS

On my drive home, my head ached, my shoes felt two sizes too small and my stomach was in knots. I don't remember driving. All I could think about were the words Michael spoke to me and the story that Pastor Jonah had told me.

It seems that Talitha and Jonah were totally smitten with each other. They had been since they were little children. When she was all of 7 years old and Jonah was 13, at a church picnic a group of children were playing close to the pond and pushed Talitha in. Of course, she couldn't swim but her lungs were in good enough working condition for her to holler out, "Jonah!" No sooner had she said those words than he appeared, jumped into the water, and pulled her to safety.

She was soaking and shivering but when her mother tried to take her from Jonah's arms, she wouldn't let go of his neck. He ended up carrying her all the way home and when he laid her down on her grandmother's bed she looked up and said in a quiet voice, "Thank you." He just smiled and kissed her on her forehead. As he was walking out of the room, Talitha called his name. He turned to see what she wanted and she said, "I love you." He grinned sheepishly and ran from the room.

That was the beginning. As they grew, they became inseparable and very connected. She knew when he needed her and he knew when she needed him. They sat together in

Sunday School and made sure they sat together during service. When they were helping out in the fields, he never let her carry anything too heavy. And, absolutely no one was ever allowed to call her anything but her given name.

When Talitha turned 10, they had a big birthday party. She was born premature and this marked a milestone for her family because the doctors had predicted she wouldn't make it past 3 years of age. They were all eating and having a great time. The children were playing, the grown-ups were talking and the dogs were all over the yard.

Talitha had mentioned that she wanted a necklace for her birthday. Jonah presented her with a plain brown box. Excitedly, she took it from his hand and sat down on the ground to open it. When she pulled the top off, her breath caught in your chest. There it was, exactly as she pictured it, a string of white pearls with the gold clasp. She looked up at Jonah and smiled. He had remembered and she was the happiest little 10 year old in Limon County Parish.

As time went on, Jonah realized that his heart ached for Talitha. He determined that one day he would marry her. When Jonah was 18, he put on his best clothes, shined his shoes so that they reflected the slightest hint of light, picked some flowers from the garden and started down the road to pay a visit to Talitha's parents.

When he arrived at their home, Talitha was out in the front yard sweeping. She grinned from ear to ear and prepared herself to receive the bouquet of flowers he held in his right hand. But, that was not to be.

Jonah marched right past her nodding his head and simply saying, "Evn'n Talitha." When he reached the front door he gave himself the once over to make sure he was still presentable and then knocked on the door. Talitha's mother, Ruth, answered the door and Jonah shyly presented the flowers to her.

He asked if he could speak with her and Talitha's daddy about, "a very impot'nt matter." Smiling, Ruth invited him in and went to the back door to call in her husband. As they all gathered around the small table, Jonah cleared his throat, sat up straight and began the speech of his life.

"I 'spect y'all know I luv Talitha. She a 'ral special girl an' in my heart. I luv her more'n anything. I want to axe if it be okay we get married. I promise to take 'ral good care of her and never lay a han' on her 'cept in luv."

They both looked at each other and then without hesitation Ruth rose from her chair and gave him a hug. That was his cue that he was now betrothed to Talitha. The only matter remaining was to ask her. As he strode purposefully to the front door he thanked God silently that all had gone well. Now, he just had to let Talitha know.

She was sitting in the front yard under the big tree. Her face was dark with anger and her mouth was set in a hard line. How dare Jonah walk right past her with flowers, why didn't he stop and speak with her? Why would he treat her like that?

As Jonah approached the tree he noticed the anger and became unnerved. Anything was better than having Talitha angry with him. So, he did what any man in that situation would do— he pulled out the promise bracelet he had for her, dropped down on one knee and presented it to her.

She sat, staring at it with raised eyebrows. Then, suddenly recognition began to dawn on her features. She sat up and cleared her throat. "You got sumpin ta say?"

Jonah's head snapped up and he hurriedly spoke the words. "Talitha, I don' axed your parents fo your han' and they said it be okay.

Now, I come to axe if you'd be my wife. Ya know I luv ya and you has my heart. Say yes. Will ya?"

Her intention was to make him sweat but her heart won out and she flung her arms around his neck loudly saying yes to his proposal. All that next year they spent lots of time together planning and preparing for their life.

They had plenty of help building a small home not far from Martha Mary's house. It had only three rooms; the bedroom, kitchen and then a big room for everything else. Talitha spent hours painting pictures that would hang on the walls of her new home; she sewed everything from sheets to table doilies.

Jonah went about setting up the garden, putting little touches on the house such as flower pots under the windows, shutters to keep out the sun in the summer and the cold in the winter, and setting up a partition in the kitchen for their bathing area.

On an especially warm spring night, after working hard all day, they found themselves down by the pond holding hands in the moonlight. They kissed one another lightly on the lips and soon they were in a full embrace. It is safe to estimate that was the night they conceived little Jonah.

When they knew that Talitha was "in the family way" Jonah forbid her doing any hard work and she definitely could not carry anything too heavy. Since the wedding date was already set, the families were not too displeased and joined in spoiling Talitha.

It was during this time that one of Talitha's little brothers decided to test his strength against that of nature. She was in the house painting when she heard a very loud scream from down by the river. She raced to the back door to see what had happened and saw the other children screaming and shouting.

Her brother, in a foolish attempt to see how far he could wade out in the water before the current caught him, was in deep trouble. He was being swept down stream by the current and couldn't swim at all. She cried out for help and ran down to the stream.

There was no hope for it but that she would have to race down the bank and try to cut him off before he ran into serious trouble. You see, at the peak of the river was a very dangerous bed of rocks. They were sharp and there were many of them. Even good swimmers had met their fate there.

As Talitha raced down the bank, news of the ordeal reached Jonah. He flew out of the field and ran as hard as he could to the stream. As he reached the stream, he saw Talitha plunge into the icy cold water and grab hold of her little brother.

The current was strong but she was determined that it would not claim him. She yanked him hard by the arm and the current did the rest. But, while it shoved him to safety it pulled her into the dangerous path of the rocks. Soon, another splash could be heard as Jonah jumped into the water and caught Talitha by her hair. It was the only thing he could reach and so he held onto it with all his might despite her screams of pain.

He could see the rock bed up ahead and with everything in him, he yanked, he twisted, he turned and he pulled to change positions. As they approached the rock bed, they shifted positions in the current. What saved them from being swept under was Jonah's leg being caught on the jagged edge of a large rock. As the pain soared through him, he held onto Talitha for dear life. He might die but his beloved would not be a sacrifice on these rocks.

Just before he passed out from pain and sheer exhaustion the other men threw a rope to them that he tied anxiously around Talitha's chest. As they pulled on the rope she held onto him with all of her might and soon they were on the bank. Jonah was out cold and she was screaming from the fear of having lost him. As the others drug her away, they lifted Jonah and took him to the house.

The doctor was sent for and as they waited for his arrival they gathered together and prayed to God for a miracle. After the doctor had examined Jonah he came out to announce his findings.

Yes, Jonah would live. Yes, Jonah would survive the pneumonia that would surely set in his lungs. But, he wasn't sure whether his leg would heal properly. The rock had cut so deep it almost severed the leg at the knee. He had done the best he could in setting it and they would have to keep a close eye on it in case infection set in.

Talitha was undaunted. She would attend her Jonah and nurse him back to health. "That,' the doctor stated, "could not be." She was "in the family way" and needed to rest her body after that harrowing ordeal. Up stepped Martha Mary assuring Talitha that Jonah was in good hands.

It took almost two months for Jonah to win his battle against the pneumonia and another three for him to be able to put any weight at all on his torn leg. Just as the decision to put off the wedding was being reached, Jonah hobbled out of the bedroom. He moved slow and unsteady but declared he would be ready for his wedding day.

The story of the love that sustained Jonah and Talitha is one that even the most adamant opponent to true love could never deny. Many were the trials but their love overcame them. Many were the struggles but their love made them bearable.

All in all, they were married for some 60 years, had 10 children, 30 grandchildren and many great and great, great grandchildren. They endured the years together until Jonah was called home by God in his 75th year. It wasn't a hard death; he simply went to sleep and never woke.

Talitha was lost without him but determined to keep on keepin' on because she had children and plenty of love to go around. And so, she was brought into the limelight with the death of her great, great grandson.

She was catapulted onto the scene by tragedy. Little Talitha was the little old lady sitting on the front row of the large sanctuary at Calvary Temple dabbing at her eyes. I would never have known it was her.

I must confess my head was beginning to ache with the twists and turns this story was taking. What was being taught to me was more than I could fathom yet I couldn't let go of it.

CHAPTER
11

WE HOLD THESE TRUTHS TO BE SELF-EVIDENT, DOESN'T APPLY!

Walking onto the stage, I felt an air of expectancy. But, there was also pent up emotion, caged energy. It felt as if they all were just waiting for the word and they would leap into action. Follow whatever path was pointed out.

I walked to the microphone and just stood. My mind didn't seem able to form the words that I needed to express my passion. As I stood there, I focused on a little brown face. Her eyes were wide but her brow was furrowed as she tried to grasp just why all these people were so excited. Her arms were wrapped tightly around her Daddy's leg and she was digging her heel into the grass. She looked up at me, blinked her eyes and then smiled the most brilliant smile. She was a picture of purity, innocence, and hope.

Before I understood what I was doing, I walked to the edge of the stage and held out my hand to her. The crowd, already quiet, grew silent. She looked up and tightened her hold on her Daddy's leg. He glanced at me, then reached down and lifted her up to me.

With her in my arms, I walked back to the microphone. She laid her head on my shoulder and I kissed the top of her head. "And a little child shall lead them," I barely whispered as I tilted my head towards the sky.

"I hold in my arms a representative of the very reason we are gathered here today. We are losing our future. Not just to violence, drugs, miseducation, assimilation, and negligence. We are losing our children because of stereotypical ignorance. The kind of thing that happens when a young black female is abused because the naturalness of her sway is mistaken for an invitation. The kind of thing that takes place when a young black male is accosted because the inherent set of his jaw is mistaken for insolence and/or unmerited pride. The kind of thing that happens when our children believe they are perfectly free to roam this land and be who they want to be because, after all, doesn't the very foundation of this country guarantee it? Does not the one document that everyone celebrates each 4th of July declare all men are created equal? Yet "we hold these truths to be self-evident" doesn't exactly come to

135

their rescue when it is assumed they are in the wrong neighborhood."

I backed away from the microphone to let my emotions slow down. Racing through me was indignation because I knew that even though I could stand quoting the constitution, the words of this document alone would never be enough to help me surface from the drowning tide that was and still is pure hatred.

I was only supposed to come out and kick off this gathering. I was supposed to walk out on that stage and introduce others that were seemingly more important and better known to guide the tide. It was my duty to bring those already in the national scheme of things out and let them shine lights into the darkness that had enveloped us all.

Yet, it was my assignment to step out of the shadows. Truly, there is no explaining just how I stood in that spot only that I knew I was supposed to stand in that spot.

My Sunday Drives

Eyes have not seen, ears have not heard, neither has it entered into the heart what God has in store for those who love Him and are called according to His purpose.

CHAPTER
12

PSYCHIATRIST
OR ANOINTING OIL?

Late Monday evening I heard the garage door open and the familiar sound of my husband's car. I was happy. I ran out to the garage, threw my arms around his neck and showered him with kisses. Although we'd only been apart a short time, I had missed him thoroughly.

Telling my husband just what I'd been up to was no easy task. He was used to my eccentricities but this one stumped him. I remember the look in his eye. My feeling was that at any moment he would snatch me up and rush me to the nearest medical facility for a complete mental evaluation.

"Sweetie, I want to talk with you about something. You know all of these drives I've been taking lately, well; I believe that I've really stumbled across something. No, stumbled would be the wrong word. I truly believe that my path has been directed and I've come across a miracle of time."

My husband sat facing me. Not just his head, but his whole body was turned towards me. His eyes were locked onto mine and his whole demeanor said, "I'm here and I'm listening." That was one thing I truly loved and appreciated about this man. Whenever I said I wanted or needed to talk with him, I got his undivided attention. However, at this moment he was staring at me with a look of confusion and concern clouding his every feature.

"Okay, honey. Continue," he said after he picked my hand up from the table and placed it in between his two, strong hands.

"Well, you remember about 4 weeks ago I woke up on Sunday and decided I wanted to go for a drive and just enjoy being out and about?"

"Hunh. Huh. I believe I do."

"Well, I believe I've really discovered something. You see, Sweetie, about 4 hours from here there is a place called Limon County Parish and I've met some very sweet and interesting people there. The thing is, I have become friends with people who by my calculation are over 150 years old. There is one person in particular, Pastor Jonah, who I've come to love, respect, admire and count as a friend."

By this time my husband was staring at me with sheer disbelief on his face. He knew that I had a very good mind but right about now he was thinking just how he could get me to the nearest psychiatrist or pull out the anointing oil and pray over me until I came back to my senses.

"Sweetie, this is no joke. I am telling you that I've run across some sort of time continuum. I drove 4 hours and turned onto County Road 420 and what I've discovered there has changed me forever. I understand much better now exactly what it was our people had to struggle against. I no longer resent the stories that seemed so degrading about my female ancestors. Stories of being raped and bearing offspring for their slave masters, being washer women, breastfeeding the children that would grow up and demand to be called mistress or master, and being called "mammy" by everyone and their brother too!'

"Do you know that they did hold family values? They never wanted to be separated, sold away from each other, or have someone else raise their children. They wanted the typical family structure– father, mother and children. They wanted their children to be educated and to have better lives. They wanted to be able to work and be paid fairly so they could pay off their debts and no longer be under the thumb of the establishment.'

"Honey, what I've come to know is that even in their state of oppression they were still striving to better themselves, provide for their families, educate their children and hold to family values. Their strength is undeniable. Honestly, there is no way that anyone from our generation could stand up under the kind of pressure they had to endure.'

"What I've learned from these beautiful people is that no matter what the situation is, never give up on the Almighty because He can work miracles even when we are in a state that we consider to be hopeless."

I sat silent because I felt myself becoming angry and passionate over this subject. The lesson that I had learned was burning within me and I wanted to share it with the one person I believed would also understand it as I did.

"So, what you're telling me is that you've been driving to this place 4 hours from here and interacting with people who by all calculations should be dead. What you are telling me is that 4 hours from here is a place not shown on any map and that no one besides you knows exists." When he finished speaking, he had a very worried look on his face and I could tell that he had already begun to pray silently for me.

At that point, my heart sank. I was causing him concern, pain. I obviously wasn't doing a very good job of communicating. I got up from the kitchen table and went into my office. I grabbed all my notes, my tape recorder, young Jonah's obituary, and anything else that I had that I could show him. As I walked back down the hall I began to pray. Silently, I prayed that God would enable me to tell this story in a way that would not upset my husband but in would cause him to understand the miracle that I'd been given.

As I entered the kitchen, I found him making coffee. Because it was so late, that could only mean one thing. He was prepared to stay up all night and work through this situation. I sat patiently at the table waiting for him to fix his first cup. As I watched him, the tension displayed in his shoulders and the set of his jaw indicated that he was highly concerned. I knew that I had some serious talking to do. I started praying again.

Once he had a very large mug filled with coffee in his hand, he sat down at the kitchen table. After a prolonged sigh, and a few sips of coffee he turned his full attention to me again. The look on his face said, "Alright,

Honey, I'm ready for more." But what came out of his mouth was, "Continue, baby doll." So, I did.

"Sweetie, I must admit that on that first Sunday drive it was just a little strange for me. As soon as I turned onto County Road 420 the scenery changed. It just seemed so much greener. The trees seemed taller and stronger. The first thing I passed was a church. It looked as if it had just been built. Church was letting out and I sat there waiting for some black faces to come through the doors but it never happened. So, I decided to just keep driving. That's when I made a right turn and met Pastor Jonah. Babe, I really think you should listen to this tape because then maybe you'll stop looking at me as if I'm having a mental breakdown. Okay? Listen."

And with that I pressed play on my little hand held recorder and watched my husband's face turn from utter despair to mild amusement. The voice of Pastor Jonah played clear and it only took a moment before you could imagine being in his presence.

Four hours later, my husband had consumed 1 pot of coffee but was visibly not quite as shaken and concerned as before. I had told him all about Pastor Jonah, Martha Mary, Little Talitha, and the wonderful Women's Day Celebration at which I'd been invited to speak.

However, there was one detail that I'd failed to reveal and I was dreading talking about it. I knew my man well, and I knew that once he heard these details my little trips back in time would either be totally forbidden or chaperoned— by him!

CHAPTER
13

THE CEMETERY
SPEAKS VOLUMES

After speaking with Pastor Jonah and learning that the young man who was shot and killed in Celebration was Talitha's great, great grandson I decided that before I left Limon County Parish I would visit the cemetery. I wanted to see the grave of Pastor Jonah's grandson and find some sort of connection.

The cemetery was located right next to Limon Parish Church. I pulled into the church parking lot and grabbed my hand held recorder before I got out of the car. As I walked through the cemetery the cool breeze helped to settle my head a little and it also felt as if God was right there with me.

I located the grave of Jonah Petersburg with little difficulty. The head stone was carved from Oak and looked as if no elements had ever touched it. On the head stone were these words, "My Beloved. Jonah Petersburg. March 5, 1803 — December 15, 1878. Husband, Father, Friend...Christian." These words had been painstakingly carved by hand. The grave had fresh flowers as if someone had just placed them there.

I sat cross legged and in deep thought at the foot of his grave. I wondered if he were alive what he would have to say about all of this. I wondered if he would stand with me at the rallies, if he would tell whoever wanted to know that no matter what the circumstance, shooting a young black man down in cold blood in the middle of the street was worse than shooting a stray dog.

I was so engrossed in my thoughts that I never heard the car pull into the parking lot. I never heard the car door open or slam shut. I never heard the footsteps of the Sheriff of Limon County Parish approaching. Not until he was standing over me, spitting tobacco out of the side of his mouth did I understand that I had company.

I jumped up so fast that I lost my balance and wound up having to grab his leg in order to keep from falling flat on my face. In that position, symbolic of servitude, I heard him say, "Nigga Gal, you outta place back here. Gal, I know ya hear me talkin', dontcha?"

And it was then that I truly came to understand the plight of black women in the deep south prior to civil rights, women's rights, or any rights. It was then that fear, anxiety and a deep hatred gripped my heart so tight I couldn't breathe.

As I got to my feet, the first thing I wanted to do was slap him so hard his momma could feel it. But, the more intelligent part of my brain prevailed and I just tried to stare a hole into his brain. He wasn't in the least affected by this and just continued spitting tobacco out of the side of his mouth with one little twist. This time he was aiming at me.

After a few seconds of this, I decided that I didn't need to try and make a stand. The best thing for me to do was start praying that God would send an angel to fight for me. And, you can believe I prayed with every fiber of my being.

People were known to disappear in these types of situations. People had been known to lose their lives when approached in this manner. People were known to have suffered dismemberment when they were thought to be "stepping out of their place." I prayed and I prayed mightily.

I glanced over at the road leading to the church and saw headlights. The car was not moving but there were three men standing beside it with long objects dangling from their hands. I could see they were watching me and the Sheriff and that didn't bode well.

There was a certain queasiness building in me. As I stood there, I was reflecting upon the many tales I'd heard, the stories I'd read, and the movies I'd watched that depicted the plight of African Americans in situations such as these. My heart was racing and my head was pounding. And all the while the words of a song kept echoing in my head. "To fight for me, I need an angel. From heaven sent falling. Jesus I'm calling an angel. I need an angel."

This overweight, middle-aged, tobacco spitting white man was hovering over me with malice in his heart. There was nothing to stop him from shooting or assaulting me. As much of a communicator as I am I couldn't put two words together at that moment. All I could do was stand still and watch this menacing man.

"Gal, I been watchin' you an' I don't thank ya know yo place. I'm here to tell ya that we don't take ta niggas drivin' fancy cars, galavantin' round like dey own de place. An' we sho' don' like no educated niggas. Get in dat fancy car an' go back to wherever it is ya came from befo' sumthin' bad happen ta ya."

When he stopped talking, he moved a step closer to me and spit tobacco directly onto my right cheek. Now, spitting is a nasty thing to begin with but you add chewed up tobacco to it and that makes it downright disgusting.

I was frozen in stunned amazement and something inside of me clicked. Something inside of me opened up and I knew that I was about to take the path that could lead to a major breakthrough in understanding or to destruction. And, at that moment either one was just fine with me.

"The bible says that we should pray for our enemies. That we should turn the other cheek. However, at this very moment I'm not hearing that. I'm hearing that you need a serious reality check. You being in that Sheriff's uniform means absolutely nothing except that you are a racist, hateful, uneducated fool with a license to carry a gun and harass blacks at will."

He stepped closer to me and I could have sworn he growled. He grabbed me by my arm and tried to throw me to the ground. Don't ask me where my strength to resist came from but I did. I pulled my arm from his grasp and continued.

"You were probably raised by a black woman because your momma was too delicate to spend the time and energy necessary to tend to you and here you stand in all of your overweight, tobacco-chewing glory threatening me. What you need is a serious beat down. Oh! Excuse me you might not understand that term. Let me say it in plain, down home English. You need to have your...."

Before I could get the rest of the words out of my mouth I saw another figure approaching. My brain started racing and I was gearing up to run full speed to my car, hop in and out run these back woods people.

The man walked up so quickly that it was almost as if he was floating. And then, recognition set in. It was the gas station attendant! That seemingly nice man that had been so helpful to me was now coming to assist "Bubba" in getting rid of me? Lord, have mercy! This was too much for me.

Tears started flowing and my whole body began shaking. Not with fear, but with the realization that one just never knew what form hatred could come in. It could look like "Bubba" or it could look like a well-meaning gas station attendant. Either way my heart was heavy.

Once he was standing next to the Sheriff, a sense of peace filled my soul. I suddenly knew that he had not come to aid in my destruction but he had come to deliver me from destruction. He had come to fight for me.

"Hello Sheriff." His voice was deep and melodic. It had a soothing quality to it and that made the Sheriff turn towards him. I stood there wiping tobacco juice from my face and trying to compose myself.

"Hey, Michael. Uh...Whatcha' doin' out here?"

"Well, Sheriff you know me. Sometimes when it's slow at the station I take a ride. I saw this young lady's car and thought she might need some help. You know she's been coming here to visit Pastor Jonah's church. She's a minister and a very nice lady. How's it going, ma'am?"

I tried to answer but nothing came out so I just nodded my head in the Sheriff's direction and gave Michael a look that said, "Please get me away from this monster." As I continued wiping my face, Michael stepped between me and the Sheriff and took me by the hand.

When he touched me all fear, anxiety and hate flew from my heart. My energy level was low, probably because my adrenaline had stopped pumping, so I leaned on Michael's arm a little heavier. He patted my hand and looked into my eyes. His look spoke to me in words that only my soul could hear. He was asking if I understood. If I knew that my angel was next to me. If I knew that God had heard my prayer and answered. I shook my head "yes" and fresh tears began falling.

He placed a hand on the Sheriff's shoulder and said, "Now, Sheriff. Why are you out here scaring this young lady? Don't you think you should be home eating dinner and spending time with the family? You know, tomorrow isn't promised and yesterday is but a vapor."

That one totally went over "Bubba's" head but I know his soul completely understood what was being said.

"Well, I...I was just tryin' ta give her some advice. I been watchin' her an'... an'...."

Suddenly the Sheriff, more affectionately known to me as "Bubba", was not so sure of himself. All the anger and malice had been drained from him and he was looking at me with new eyes. The importance of him scaring me and running me out of town faded. Now, I wasn't foolish enough to believe that he had a mind renewal, or that he had changed from his racist beliefs. But I knew that, as the old folks say, "somethin' got a hold of him" and he would not be able to function the same as usual.

"Well, it was awful nice of you to stop and offer her some friendly advice," Michael said. "But, I'm wondering just how she got that dirt on her clothes and spit on her face. Would you happen to know anything about that?"

"Bubba" turned beet red and I believe smoke started coming from his ears. It wasn't embarrassment; it was pure, unbridled anger. He was the Sheriff of this town and what was this gas station attendant doing questioning his actions. White men should stick together!

"Boy, I jus' know you ain't axing me 'bout my biznes." This was said while his hand was resting on his pistol.

Michael started walking me towards my car and as we moved past the Sheriff he looked over his shoulder and spoke to him.

"How good it is for men to dwell together in unity. The eyes of the Lord look over the world and His face is towards the righteous.

They call upon Him in their distress and He answers. Therefore, they declare, "I love the Lord for He heard my cry. I will bless Him at all times. But, woe unto those that seek to destroy a child of the Most High King for then shall the King of Glory step into the battle and that one shall be utterly destroyed."

Michael stopped walking and turned around to face the Sheriff. "Thus saith the Lord of Hosts. Touch not Mine anointed. Neither do My prophets any harm. You have been weighed in the balance and found wanting. This very night your soul shall be required of you."

As I stood at the front of my car, I felt the presence of the Lord and I knew then beyond all doubt that standing beside me was an angel, sent for my deliverance. Here, standing in this place that time had forgotten God was showing me just how much He loved me. God had heard my cry. He had answered my prayer. And I know that had it not been for the Lord on my side, raising up a standard against the evil one I would have lost my life this very night. I couldn't hold back the tears and praise was on the tip of my tongue. "My God, my God," was all that I could manage to say.

The Sheriff was visibly shaken. Although he tried to hold onto his anger and dignity, anyone watching would have been able to tell that he was not as confident as he was trying to portray. As Michael turned away from him. "Bubba" turned towards the car and the men waiting on the road. He lifted his hand to them and gestured that it was over, there would be no action tonight.

In a last ditch effort to salvage himself, "Bubba" opened his car door, stood with one foot resting on the runner and his arm draped across the door. He addressed Michael, "Boy, you betta' watch yo'self. We run Limon County Parish." Then he got into the patrol car, started it up and drove up to meet with "the boys."

With tears streaming down my face and a snotty nose I embraced Michael. I held onto him with all that I had and cried. I cried because I had just been supernaturally delivered. I cried because I'd never in all of my life experienced such hatred. I cried because God had sent my angel to me.

Michael held me in his arms and with a soothing voice calmed me down. "It's over now. God has delivered you and because of this you will be a stronger vessel. He has begun a good work in you and will continue it until the glorious return of His Son. Just as Nehemiah rebuilt the walls of Jerusalem and Joshua brought down the walls of Jericho, through this amazing experience you will also be an instrument for building up and tearing down. Listen for the voice of God and He will direct your path and open your understanding. And always remember, He will keep you in perfect peace as long as you keep your mind stayed on Him."

With that said Michael kissed me on my forehead, helped me get into my car, told me to drive carefully, closed my door and walked away.

As I drove away from the church, I could see three sets of headlights in my rear view mirror... Michael's, Sheriff "Bubba", and his three hench men. I pushed play on the Cd player and started singing along with John P. Kee: "If there be anyone who's going through. We have the answer for you. Trust and obey and never give in. Only the strong shall survive and win. If there is no sign, keep this in mind. He'll show up on time." Amen!

CHAPTER
14

BUBBA, THE ANGEL, AND A PISSED OFF SISTAH!

My husband actually had a smile on his face. I had been able to record a portion of the church service at Pastor Jonah's and he loved the singing. I told him about the women praying over me and how I felt as if I were going through a rite of passage.

We both laughed when I talked about how Martha Mary and Pastor Jonah reacted to my SUV. I felt as if I was communicating well and he understood the importance of this miracle.

He asked me about the little town. He asked me to describe the church and the houses. He asked me to tell him about the gas station and the attendant. Then he asked the one question I truly didn't want to answer. He asked if I'd run into any trouble.

"Honey, you're a good looking black woman. Educated." And with a slight smile he stated, "Opinionated."

I thought about elbowing him but then, the truth is the truth!

"Driving a nice car all alone in a place where civil rights hasn't even been thought about. No one said anything to you? No one tried anything with you? The white folks were cool with you? Honey, Tell me. Did anything happen that I should know about?" And it was at that very point he started looking me up and down.

He was taking inventory and trying to see any tell-tale signs of injury. I had no visible bruises but the mental ones were there and I was glad he couldn't see inside my mind.

I guess I took too long answering because the next thing I knew his face got dark with concern. I know the look on my face must have shown my desire to avoid this topic. He scooted his chair out from the kitchen table, took hold of my chair and pulled me closer to him.

That wasn't a very comfortable position; it left me no squirming room. So, I leaned forward, placed a light kiss on his lips and asked if we could move into the den and continue this discussion.

After getting settled on the love seat in the den, he said, "Alright honey let me hear it." So, I started cautiously to tell about my experience that evening in the cemetery at Limon Parish Church.

"Sweetie, after talking with Pastor Jonah about young Jonah's funeral and learning the whole story about the family, I decided to drive over to the cemetery. All I wanted to do was see the head stone, sit in peace and solitude and gather my thoughts. But, it turned out to be one of the worst decisions I've ever made." I stopped talking then bowed my head.

The image of the Sheriff looming over me, grabbing me, spitting tobacco in my face and making me feel less than a human was overwhelming. Remembering how sore my arm was that night, how my whole body was tense and I couldn't fall into a peaceful sleep made my shoulders tense. A single tear slid down my cheek and I buried my head in my husband's chest.

That was all it took for him to get upset. There were a few things he just didn't tolerate. And one of those things just happened to be seeing tears falling from my eyes. It bothered me, because I knew what he was thinking and I knew that he was totally, undeniably and thoroughly pissed.

Before I continued with my story, I did my best to compose myself. I slid into his arms with my back to his chest so that I wouldn't have to see his face and know that I was upsetting him.

As I was settling myself, he tightened his arms around me and pulled me as close as he possibly could to him. He gently laid his head next to mine and kissed my ear. We sat quietly that way until I was ready to continue talking.

I took a deep breath and continued. "Well, you know me. I was sitting there totally lost in my own little world and I never heard the car pull into the lot. I never heard anything. It wasn't until he was standing over me that I knew I was in trouble. You know what? The worst feeling you can have is to be totally at the mercy of another person. You don't know if you are going to make it to the next sunrise or if you'll make it but only part of you. That big, tobacco chewing, gun toting white man was standing over me and talking junk. Now, you know I don't like to be spoken to just any kind of way but in this situation I was too scared to even put a sentence together. And, when I looked around and saw "the boys" just waiting for their signal to join the party, I really got anxious and started praying. I was praying so hard because I didn't have any experience with this kind of stuff. All I could remember were the movies, the books, the stories I've heard all my life about blacks losing their lives just because they had "stepped out of place" and pissed some white person off." I paused because my heart was pounding, my head was hurting and I was "feeling" this just a little too much.

I finally spit out the whole story. The more details I told about "Bubba", the more my husband got upset and I could feel him growing protective and vengeful. When I started telling him about Michael, I felt the same release in him that I'd felt in the presence of Michael. He seemed to relax his arms, his breathing became deeper and I could feel a sense of peace come over him.

That's when I began to relax. Yes, I'm an independent, strong willed, vivacious, "don't even think about it!" kind of woman but I also loved my husband deeply. I respected his feelings and his thoughts. I never wanted to cause him pain or discomfort. And when I did in some way bring him pain my strongest desire at that very moment was to relieve it. To somehow, make it all better. So, you can only imagine my relief when I felt him start to relax.

I have to be honest. I was also very worried about his reaction and the possibility of my being unceremoniously yanked off my little blessed excursions to Limon County

Parish. So, my being able to make his pain go away was a win, win situation for everyone.

The more I talked about Michael, the more I could feel him relax. So, I continued telling him how Michael came and helped me back to my car and those wonderful words he spoke to me. "It's over now. God has delivered you and because of this you will be a stronger vessel. He has begun a good work in you and will continue it until the glorious return of His Son. Just as Nehemiah rebuilt the walls of Jerusalem and Joshua brought down the walls of Jericho, through this amazing experience you will also be an instrument for building up and tearing down. Listen for the voice of God and He will direct your path and open your understanding. And always remember, He will keep you in perfect peace as long as you keep your mind stayed on Him."

That's what Michael had spoken to me. I could still hear his voice just as if he were standing there now speaking. When I repeated them to my husband I saw him staring off as if he was watching the scene take place. As if he was viewing a movie.

While he was staring into space he said, "You know, I feel such a sense of peace right now. Just you talking about it has calmed me down a lot. Honey, how did you feel when you knew that God had sent an angel to rescue you? Did you get a chance to ask him anything?"

"No, Sweetie. I really was too much in awe and just plain ready to get out of "Bubba's" territory. But, now that you mention it, there are so many things I would have loved to ask Michael. But, he had given me such a spirit of peace that I wasn't anxious over anything. It was just like how I feel when I've been running and running and finally my opportunity comes to sink into a hot tub and soak. I just wanted to bask in that moment. I was just thankful for the respite. Oh!

Sweetie, guess what Michael said to the Sheriff."

"What?"

I lay back with my eyes closed and repeated the words of Michael concerning Sheriff "Bubba." "How good it is for men to dwell together in unity. The eyes of the Lord look over the world and His face is towards the righteous. They call upon Him in their distress and He answers. Therefore, they declare, "I love the Lord for He heard my cry. I will bless Him at all times." But, woe unto those that seek to destroy a child of the Most High King for then shall the King of Glory step into the battle and that one shall be utterly destroyed. Thus saith the Lord of Hosts, Touch not mine anointed. Neither do my prophets any harm. You have been weighed in the balance and found wanting. This very night your soul shall be required of you."

We were both quiet for a while just thinking about those words. There are times when you should take heed. I would think that having an angel speak to you would be one of those times.

Whether or not the Sheriff knew that Michael was sent by God or that his words were penned by God was up for grabs. I don't think he was that in tune with God and he certainly wasn't concentrating of being pleasing in His sight. After a while I asked, "Babe, how would you feel if someone said that to you?"

CHAPTER
15

NOT THE END OF THE ROAD

"To everything there is a season and a time to every purpose under the heaven: A time to be born and a time to die; A time to plant and a time to pluck up that which is planted; A time to kill and a time to heal; A time to break down and a time to build up; A time to weep and a time to laugh; A time to mourn and a time to dance; A time to cast away stones and a time to gather stones together; A time to embrace and a time to refrain from embracing; A time to get and a time to lose; A time to keep and a time to

cast away; *A time to rend and a time to sew; A time to keep silence and a time to speak; A time to love and a time to hate; A time of war and a time of peace.*" *Ecclesiastes 3: 1-8*

Driving down the road to Martha Mary's house, I knew that my time in Limon County Parish was coming to an end. It sent a pain streaking through my heart because I had come to love, respect, cherish and appreciate these people.

My gratitude to God for granting me this miracle of time was unexplainable. The wisdom that I'd already garnered was incredible and I wanted to continue growing through this experience.

In my head, I knew it was time to say goodbye to these beloved people. In my heart, I was reluctant to let go and mourning the loss already.

As usual, the children were outside playing when I reached Martha Mary's little house. I was trying to spot my little friend, Talitha, but didn't see those two ponytails flying around the yard.

When I pulled into the yard the children stopped playing and ran over to my car door. They were dark skinned beauties. Their features would be considered plain or average by most but to me they were objects of exquisite, undefiled beauty. They had a radiance that shined through like sunshine breaking through the window in the morning. They were clean, dressed neatly, barefoot and full of energy.

I got out of the car and hugged each child. Then I leaned down and asked, "Is your grandmother at home?" They giggled because according to them I sounded "white". They pointed towards the house all saying in chorus, "Yes!"

I walked towards the door and as I did, I could hear crying. That was unusual so I hurried my steps and arrived just in time to see Talitha rip a picture from the wall and fall to the floor holding it and crying uncontrollably. I stood there with my eyes stretched wide in amazement.

As I stepped through the door, she heard my footstep and raised her head just enough to see who had come through the door. When she saw it was me, a red flush came over her face and she immediately sat up. As I glanced from Talitha to Ruth to Martha Mary I was at a loss because I'd never seen this kind of behavior in this home.

Ruth knelt down beside Talitha, gently rubbed the little girl's head and then in a very hoarse tone said, "Baby, don't act like dat. You did a good job. Don't be hurt cuz the color ain't to your likin'."She sat down on the floor and pulled Talitha into her lap.

Martha Mary turned to me and said, "De chile jus' upset cuz she don' have de right color. Say she wanna gibe de bes' ta God."

I stood wondering just what I could do to help Talitha. I knew the feeling. I'd been there done that. Wanting to give your absolute best to God but feeling as if you had somehow only achieved average. It's amazing though how when we feel that we aren't giving our best God steps in and shows us how much He loves our faith and determination. And, He takes what we have offered up to Him and works miracles. Little becomes much in the hands of the Master.

I knelt down beside her and touched her head. I began to tell her the story of this little girl that I once knew. She grew up in the church. As a matter of fact, her father was the pastor of the church. She sang in the choir, played the part of Mary 2 years in a row in the Christmas Play, and was even into soccer and volleyball at school. But, she never quite felt that she was making the grade. When she became a teenager, she started singing more and was even asked to sing at some very important events. She was asked, at the age of 16, to sing with a college choir. But even then she didn't feel that she was giving her very best.

Self-conscious. Always afraid that someone would notice a hair out of place, something hanging from her nose, a run in her stockings or (God forbid) something wrong with her clothing. When she opened her mouth to sing, the butterflies in her stomach could have populated an open field. And, to hear herself singing on tape was pure torture.

Finally, she hit womanhood. Those first few years were filled with doubt and anxiety. But one night as she was preparing to deliver a message at church the next day she heard a little voice speaking to her heart.

She was sitting there frantically trying to make her message into something that it was not, should not be. As she sat with her head cradled in her hands, rocking back and forth from frustration and exhaustion the Spirit of the Lord came to her.

He told her that He was well pleased with what she was doing. Not because she hit those notes right on and not because all of her messages were typed and pleasing to the eye. He was well pleased with her because her desire was to please Him. It touched Him because she earnestly wanted nothing less than to be a woman after the heart of God.

He told her to just continue being faithful and to always send up her offering from a heart filled with praise. After that night, she no longer feared not giving her best. She only kept her faithfulness and her heart was always filled with praise.

"God is an understanding God. He knows our thoughts and though we might not be pleased with what we have done for Him, He can take it, use it and touch the heart of someone. All God wants is our commitment to Him; our desire to be like His Son, Jesus Christ. For us to walk by faith knowing that we can do all things through Him for He is our strength and our provider. Talitha, this picture that you are so displeased with is beautiful in the eyes of God because it came straight from a heart filled with pure desire to please Him. It came from your heart and believe me when I say that God is smiling right now because in His eyes it is a precious gift."

Talitha was listening intently. She cocked her head to the side and asked me through tear filled eyes, "Who was that little girl you were talking about?"

I smiled at her and said, "That little girl was me."

She put her arms around my neck and gave me the biggest squeeze. As we hugged, I felt such love for this little one. She was truly precious in my sight. I suggested, "Let's take a walk." Talitha slid from her mother's lap and said, "Okay."

As we were going through the door, I looked back at Ruth who was standing next to Martha Mary smiling. She mouthed, "Thank you." I just winked at her and continued on through the door.

Talitha and I decided we wanted to walk down by the river. We held hands and talked as if we hadn't a care in the world. I was touched by her wisdom and her heart of gold. She told me that she drew the pictures because they helped her to show how wonderful God is. She wanted everyone to appreciate His creations.

As we walked by the side of the river she asked, "Why is it people nevah 'preciate beauty 'til it's too late? Dey walk by it ev'ry day but jus' don't seem ta see it. I 'member Pastor Jonah sayin' God created ev'ything. Don't dat make ev'ything beautiful?"

Since I had been walking around not seeing the beauty of everything, I had to take a moment to evaluate just how true her statement was. And, it was abundantly true.

How beautiful is green grass? You know that kind that feels like carpet and looks so shiny and green you want to just sit and bask in it. How beautiful is a 100 year old tree? That tree that has been rooted in the same spot for so long it has become a landmark and a part of the town's history. How beautiful is it to see the heat rising from the pavement and the hazy shadows it casts as a result?

This world is filled with beauty and usually in our haste to get through the day, reach our destination ahead of schedule or complete a task that has been hounding us; we walk right by it and never give it a second glance. So, as I answered her I began to look around and see just how excellent God's creation was.

"Yes. God made everything and that does make it beautiful. In Genesis it tells us that God made everything and when He finished He looked around and saw that it was good, in fact very good. We shouldn't just walk by His creations and never give them a second glance. We should, every day, at least appreciate two things that God has given us and thank Him for those things. Your pictures are a testament to God's wonderful creations. Would you do me a big favor?"

"Yes, Ma'am," replied Talitha.

"I would love it if you would draw me a picture that I could take home with me. Would you do that?"

"Yes, Ma'am. I will."

As we reached the bank of the river, I decided that we would stop here and have a seat. I wanted to have a talk with Talitha uninterrupted and prayerfully memorable. We sat on the bank, took off our shoes and let our feet rest in the cool water. I took her hand in mine and began rubbing it gently.

"Talitha, there are some things that I'd like to share with you. Even in this time that you are growing up you can be what you want and need to be. There are no limitations other than the ones we put on ourselves. I know that people tell you women have their place and they should not step out of it, but look at the women in the Bible. They were leaders, way makers, and messengers. Some ran their own businesses."

I continued, "The first eyes laid on the risen Savior belonged to women and they were the ones that He told to go and tell His disciples that He was risen. They carried the news of the Messiah raised from the dead. What I'm trying to tell you is that you can be an instrument for God's use as long as you develop your talents and abilities and then yield them to the Master. Please, think about every step that you take. All of your steps should take you closer to God, never further away from Him. Every step you take should enable you to use what the Master has given you more with each passing day. Never hide your gifts because then you don't affect anyone for the kingdom. And, I want you to know that I've come to genuinely love and care for you. I always pray for you and keep you close in my heart." After saying that, I reached over and gave her a huge hug. I couldn't believe that I would have to leave this place and this wonderful little girl. My heart was aching and all I wanted to do was burst into shameless tears."

"Lord, help me," I whispered because I needed Him. I needed Him.

Walking back to Martha Mary's was silent. In one pair of hands we held our shoes and with the other pair of hands we held onto each other. Inside of mine, her hand was so small and slight. I felt as if I needed to protect her from the storms raging all around her and give her the chance that every human being deserves. The chance to succeed in life. We finally turned into the yard and there sat Pastor Jonah, Martha Mary and some others whose faces were familiar but names were not.

That toothless grin began shining and as always it brought a smile to my face. He stood up and offered me his chair. "Been walkin", hey? Pretty out deh, ain't it?"

I nodded my head absently. My mind was desperately trying to wrap itself around the concept of leaving these people. I didn't want to cry but I could feel the tears welling up and so I closed my eyes and bowed my head.

True to their nature, everyone sitting there bowed their heads and began saying, "Yes, Lawd!" in preparation to pray. I had had no intention at of issuing forth a prayer but then my Pastor had always said to be prepared at ALL times.

Alright, to obey was better than to sacrifice.

"Father, here I sit with these beautiful and blessed people. Those whom You created and love more than we can even try to understand. It's here that I sit to ask You to please send your angels to watch over them. Let Your arm of protection stretch from home to home, from person to person. Honor them with Your peace and let Your grace and mercy walk daily by their sides. Lord, bless the children with good health and great minds. Let them grow up to fear and reverence You as their parents and grandparents do. Provide them the opportunity to show just how marvelous the works of Your hands are by always letting their lights shine for You. Walk all through Limon County Parish and then Father, when You've finished taking care of all Your people, I ask that You to come and see about me. Hold me up with Your powerful hand, guide me with Your finger of love, grant me peace according to your loving kindness. Touch me from the crown of my head to the soles of my feet and remove anything that is not like or of You and replace it with all that

I need to run this race, to endure until the end. My God, grant me serenity and place in my hands the tools to help me fight the good fight of faith so that one day I might see Your glorious face and fall at Your feet to worship throughout the ceaseless ages of eternity. Father, I know that You are able to do above and beyond all that I'm asking and because I know that, I give You the glory, the honor and the praise. And, I say....Thank You Lord."

As I sat there with my head bowed, the tears now flowed freely but it was not out of place. Those around me were praising God with tears, with shouts of "Glory!", "Amen, Amen!", and "Please, Master please." It was so exhilarating and I'd not experience anything like this in ages and ages. So, I sat back and basked in the presence of the Holy Spirit.

Giving Pastor Jonah a ride back home was a delight. He was in such a jovial mood and it rubbed off on me. We laughed about the time Talitha came running into the yard screaming because one of the "bad" roosters had decided to hop on top of her head and hold on. She was screaming and running in place. I laughed, but I know had that been me I'd have been doing the same thing!

We also talked about how Martha Mary continually grins at Brother Brown. "Now, come on," I said to Pastor Jonah. "What's wrong with a woman smiling every once in a while. Does it always have to be we're smiling up on a brother? There is such a thing as just greeting a person." This was said with a wide grin and the most devious shine my eyes could muster.

Pastor Jonah sat further back in the seat, turned his head towards me, sighed heavily and burst into laughter. So did I.

Laughter did heal the soul, add to your life, and heal the body. But, when I saw Pastor Jonah's house coming into view it slowed my heart down and that heaviness returned. You know the kind that sits on your heart like a brick and won't move no matter what you do. I had decided to not mention that I wasn't planning on returning to Limon County Parish so I was all set to do my best impression of the returning guest.

As we sat in front of that weather worn house, I took Pastor Jonah's hand and turned towards him. "Pastor Jonah you are one of the most blessed men I know. I want to thank you for allowing me to speak at your Women's Day program. I've meant to do so for some time now but it just kept slipping my mind. You will never know how much that meant in my life, in my ministry. Have I told you how much you remind me of my grandfather? He was a gentle and kind man. He owned a candy store. You know, I'm surprised I don't have more cavities because I used to eat so much candy. And, he never said a word. But, anyway, thank you so much for being a kind and gentle reminder of him. Well, I guess I need to start heading home. Those clouds don't look too friendly."

"Well, chile. You head on home, now. Don' get caught in no storm 'cause 'roun des parts it can be a mess." He stepped outside of the car and I came around to his side in order to give him a hug. As my arms closed around him, he said in my ear, "You's one blessed woman a God. You keep on speakin' and servin' de Lord. He pleased wit you an' dat a good thing. I love ya."

After he said those words, it was all I could do was nod my head and give a halfhearted smile to him. I walked back around to the driver's side, opened the door and stepped inside.

As I pulled away from the house, I could see Pastor Jonah just standing there in the road. Waving and smiling that toothless grin. Was that someone standing next to him? I really didn't know if someone had come up that quick but they were waving too and I blew my horn and waved out the window.

Once I pulled back on to the main road I stopped the car on the side of the road. I got out with my digital camera and began to take pictures of the sign that announced, "Limon County Parish." I turned and took a picture of the "Andy Griffith" gas station with its gleaming red pumps and then got back into the car. Since I'd already taken pictures of everything else [the church and cemetery, Martha Mary's, the huge plantation house, the river] there was only one thing left to do. And, I did it. Reluctantly, but I did it. I got back inside of my car, adjusted myself, turned on my Cd and started the 4 hour drive home. As I passed the gas station I didn't see anyone around but a knot caught in my throat and I began to cry in earnest.

When I glanced in my rear view mirror, I could see Michael standing in the road watching me leave. And then, so quiet it was almost inaudible, I could hear someone saying to me, "Fret not. You will return again someday. Your mission has only begun - not ended. May the peace of God abide with you and His love continually shine through you. May His grace and mercy stay active in your life. Remember, in all things give thanks unto the Lord for He is worthy. And, know this......God is pleased with you."

The Cd was playing and I reached over to turn up the volume so that I could not hear one of my favorite songs but sing along with Mary, Mary. "Tragedies are common place. All kinds of diseases people are slippin' away. Economy's down, people don't get enough pay. But as for me all I can say is....Thank you Lord for all you've done for me!"

ABOUT THE AUTHOR

Apostle Yolanda Collins Dean was born August 1964 to Reverend Lawrence Collins, Sr. and Juanita McClain Collins in Rochester, New York. She is the youngest of four children. At a young age she was active in ministry using her gifts in the choir, usher board and in plays. Coming from priestly lineage, it wasn't long before she answered the call of God on her life. She was licensed in September 2000 and ordained in January 2003.

She has recorded with the Georgia State University Choir; The William Boyd Gospel Choir featured soloist on "Be Grateful"; Robbie Baxter & Higher Praise featured soloist on "Rain On Me"; She wrote & produced "Just Like Jesus", "It's Me Lord" and "I'm Comin' Out" on her debut CD.

During her time in Atlanta, Georgia she became active in the campaigns to Save Our

Children during the time when African American children were missing and murdered. She used her voice to bring peace and comfort during rallies and vigils throughout the city,

Apostle Dean is the Founder and CEO of Chosen One Ministries International. She walks with her husband, Pastor Feotis Dean at The Way of Fellowship Tabernacle.

Apostle Dean is anointed, appointed and approved of God. She knows what it is to be homeless, jobless, penniless, sick in your body while the devil was trying to steal your mind. She suffered the brutality of domestic violence. The desperation of having your loved one addicted to drugs.

Yet, she knows the awesome power of Abba's might and His ability to deliver you out of every affliction! She will be the first to tell you that serving the Lord under her mantle is no easy road; however, it is the greatest joy of her life. Because she understands the power of Jehovah's holy word, more often than not you will hear her declare, "Live in the WORD,.Let the WORD live in YOU!"

To book Apostle Yolanda Collins Dean for a ministry engagement call (407) 314-7170. Submit a prayer request, via email at chosenoneinternational@yahoo.com.

For further information on Chosen One Ministries International visit www.yolandadean.com.

Excerpt from My Sunday Drives, Vol. 2

The first glance is never the last...

It had only been 6 months since my last visit to Limon County Parish. My heart was breaking because I missed Pastor Jonah, Martha Mary and Talitha. I missed the little church that had so much love and an abundance of the Spirit. They were like family to me. Although I had given my word that I wouldn't go back there, I knew that if I didn't go I would just be hurting myself.

You know that feeling you get in the pit of your stomach that says something bad is coming your way? Well, it hit me like 2 ton of bricks. I couldn't eat, couldn't drink and I could not for the life of me seem to pick myself up and do what I'd planned for the day. I just knew that I was on my last leg and would perish soon. Then the phone rang. I looked at my caller I.D, it was a call from Limon County Parish. My heart was racing as I picked up the phone and said, "*Hello*." It was Martha Mary and the tone of her voice was so sad that I immediately plopped down in the nearest chair.